The truth about
Catherine and Felicity
and their year of 1910

THE TRUTH ABOUT
CATHERINE AND FELICITY
AND THEIR YEAR OF 1910

an epyllion by Adrian McMinn

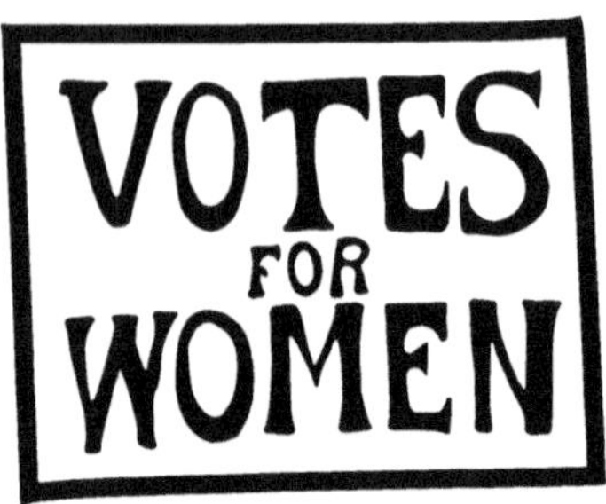

A catalogue record for this work is available from the National Library of Australia

Adrian McMinn, author.
Book Design by Bettina Kaiser, BKA+D

ISBN (hbk) 978-1-7636626-0-5
ISBN (pbk) 978-1-7636626-1-2
ISBN (ebk) 978-1-7636626-2-9

To Gift, who always asked how my novella was going
... and whose beauty is too idiosyncratic to use
for the too idiosyncratic beauty of the Contessa in Chapter 9.

To Sister Imma, who chatted from Rome to Naples
and provided me with a narrator.

To Andrew Inman, generous colleague. Our last meeting
commemorated, somewhat, on page 140.

Virtue itself turns vice, being misapplied,
And vice sometime's by action dignified.
Romeo and Juliet, II, iii, 21–22

Chapter 1.
Apologia

As the reader will see, my first chapter is not prologue or introduction but an attempt to explain this disappointing story.

I hoped to write an edifying feminist memoir of my great-aunt Catherine Dewhirst, who I believed to be a London suffragette, campaigning for the rights of women in the long ago year mentioned in my title.

A first title, The Female David, was inspired by the enthusiasm that always fills the wings of do-gooders, but it was not to be.

My title is less ambitious, identifying two friends who consorted in one year, and stands as a warning, one way or the other, that the past is not everything a seeker might wish it to be.

I wonder why I didn't abandon the project having discovered the unalterable truth … or why I decided to fling the curtains open and let the light reveal what it may, whether the folly of my heroines, or the immutable treachery of the world we call home, or, perhaps, the recklessness of your poor author.

I trust you accept my word nothing of importance will be left out, that I can be relied upon to explore my heroine's story with respect to the facts, and to the excitations of my abilities.

My pursuit of Catherine has proven to be a very rocky ride, as I have been called to places I could not have anticipated; places that are comic, unedifying and dark; places that defy the cant of ideology and lacking the characters and circumstance of a story amenable to the sensibilities of the progressive literary public.

The worst of it is the facts, which are as true as the stars above, will cause my hopes to soon leave the trail of righteousness and proceed as a narrative of dubious masquerade, and, in the fullness of time, spiral down to the most shocking depths an individual can be so misguided to willingly plumb.

Of redeeming qualities I can only offer the indomitable spirit of youth, though I am not sure that makes the story worth telling.

You may understand when I say, I am not the first adventurer to be blown off course by strange winds.

◆ ◆ ◆

I first learnt of Catherine in 1956, my thirteenth year, from a distant relative who visited our weatherboard house on the outskirts of Sydney during his stopover from a world cruise. He arrived with my English grandmother in her stolid grey British-built Morris.

I listened to the living room talk of the old days, of a world unlike my own that was inhabited by characters who fitted no type I was familiar with, about money and where it had gone, and an amusing reference to Aunt Catherine's suffragettism. I marked that word and was delighted with my school encyclopaedia's explication.

I never saw this shining young man again and, observing his accent and the anchor motif on the silver buttons of his double-breasted navy-blue jacket, I wondered what he thought of our veteran-built cottage.

I cannot account for my acuity, but I remember thinking Catherine's fleeting appearance signified the star of the show, like a comet rushing excitedly through the night sky, revealing how cold, lonely and staid the numinous really is. And perhaps it was the sensitivities of youth which had me intuiting, on this particular topic, some things were to be left unspoken.

Later, during my first working years, I would stay overnight at my grandmother's harbourside flat, listening to her reminiscences about the war years—about the Luftwaffe dropping a parachute bomb on the family tennis court, and Gran escorting old Queen Mary during her inspection of her wartime regiment, for my grandmother and her comrades were the defenders of the night skies of Manchester. I now wished I'd had the wit to be more inquiring about the relatives she mentioned; her older sister, who she felt never approved of her, and the occasional reference to Catherine, which I still remember being of an understanding yet enigmatic stripe. I feel for my grandmother now; she memorialised a distant and long-gone drizzling world, but now lived in a sun-bathed foreign land slogging as a bookkeeper in York Street, Sydney, relieved by the lively solace of a weekly episode of I Love Lucy, and occasionally by having a daft grandchild to confide in.

I took orders in the mid-1960s as a Sister of Mercy, but decamped after a decade and a succession of old popes who seemed to think their God cared too much for the mumbling of the Roman church, just as they did.

I joined a feminist group committed to reform of the gender biases of the workplace, and after a career spanning five decades I have accepted retirement.

The world has grown younger beneath this aged nun. I've witnessed the twilight of a civilisation and the withering of its icons. In its place, either obstinacy or a dumb show, and of my part in the latter ideology, which is still so righteous and irresistible, an *aria* delivered en masse to our sisters as part of the furniture of the workplace—both convincing and conniving in our consciousness-raising sessions on how to be assertive gender members. How does any cohort resist the enticements of advantage presented so convincingly, in a voice so purely without ambiguity?

I've had worrying visions of the work wrought by my hands, for what effect do our pleasing harangues have on our less righteous sisters, who surely are present, in cohorts, among the miscellany of human types who are our captive and easily persuaded audience—opportunists vulnerable to the alliances that gossip assembles, narcissi, the greedy, the natural informers and vigilant pedants, the unreflective, thieves, passive careerists, backsters, prevaricators, spies and sycophants, and the many simple travellers who are swept along and to be found attendant to anything on the upward swing … not to forget those of no higher pedigree than the dregs of the other genders.

I'm not saying it's a basket of snakes … I'm saying once more, such as these flourish in any cohort.

As I write I reflect on my early teaching years, how our curriculum for forming new minds was so indelible and thought-out, not all the experiences of a long life, nor the shenanigans of Satan himself, *would budge the borders of the Lord's property.*

I was preserved by the faith our gender aspirations had kinship with the saviour's beatitudes … but it was the wisdom of a pagan, dear sweet Virgil, who kept me grounded with a theory of everything that was both true and worth knowing. If our Christ gave the good news of a world to come, then Virgil knew the bad news about the forces that rule over us in this world and its succession of unending calamities—'for a law of nature makes all things go to the bad, lose ground and fall away.'

And so, my unenlightened self chose to pursue the historic Aunt Catherine, with the last of my health, hope and happiness, thinking she was a heroine for our times.

I wrote letters to family members and the replies produced the following facts: Catherine Dewhirst, born 1889, had grown up privileged, left her Northern home, age twenty, to study in London, and at this tender age published radical suffragette polemics in a national newspaper, before marrying well and raising a family. From this I imagined Catherine to be rebellious, independent, educated, politically radical … a goldmine.

Then a package of documents arrived, within a front-page newspaper clipping dated April 1910 with a banner headline crying 'Women's Riot', and under its black letters a striking image of the suffragette disturbances in London. The camera peers through a line of policemen, capturing a young woman standing alone amongst the detritus of riot.

She wears a long dress buttoned to the neck, laced boots, and a magnificently stylish naval bonnet with a band boldly reading **HMS** *Britannia*. With one hand she holds a placard which reads 'Votes for Women,' while her other hand points to her suffragette message.

Beyond her is the murk of oppression—policemen, dour buildings, while she is exquisitely illuminated, for the sun is only shining upon her. Below the photograph of this defiant, courageous, and righteous Female David trickles the caption, 'Miss Catherine Dewhirst, student and suffragette'.

On the back, in faded pencil, are the words I thought must be heaven-sent: 'Aunt Catherine!' … the exclamation mark is not mine.

My heart was palpitating as if something of great violence had rushed toward me and I could do nothing but surrender to it. My mind reeled, my sacred heart carried aloft like a cherub amongst the soft grey billowing clouds of a baroque church ceiling where it hovered as a downy feather, ecstatically suspended upon the air.

This was more than I expected. I felt saved from doubt.

What a feminist biography this would be, or perhaps a 400-page novel, a historical novel so padded with authentic minutiae it would write itself … culled from research and press-ganged into the service of my passion, producing page upon chapter of respectful literature!

My apostolic zeal led me to speculate about the fate of Catherine after the tumultuous year of 1910. I could only guess … persecution!

Like so many dreams, the Female David also does not exist.

I have served my isms faithfully, remained loyal to all my sisters, no matter how mad, bad, sad, and tedious to know, and never expressed doubts which would be an obstacle to our righteous march.

I have accepted the ambiguities which are commonly forced upon one. I say to you, I am blameless before the cause.

I have conformed while knowing wars are won by the big battalions – in our case, big battalions of sisters who are combed out of the rear areas by our sergeants, propagandised by our officers, and then sent back to the front, eager for opportunities to apply our ideology.

Experience tells me the following holds true of every corner of this vain old world—a new *apostle* to any coven is not long disposed of their illusions about the congregations they will stare out to from any pulpit. The congregants are the innocent, pretenders and poseurs, who find themselves alone in a bad world, and if not for the bell would wander off to an anonymous fate.

During a research trip to England I suffered my epiphany.

A newly discovered relative discoursed at length about himself, his wife, his children, and his career, as my mind wandered into a fantasy of the speaker being torn apart by daemons, he was saved—praise be to the Virgin—by the wife's subtle insubordination. She invited me to inspect the attic, where I came upon a little leather suitcase labelled in broken letters of antique gold, *Miss C. Dewhirst.*

I remember how the latches opened with a snap, and how I immediately closed them again so I might luxuriate in the gentle thud of her last closing.

The case was a relic of Catherine's schooldays but served as her personal archive—photographs, family memorabilia, and two thin journals secreted as part of the case-lining, the first in time labelled 1910, wherein I would be introduced to the amazing Felicity.

My hands shook as I opened the journal at random, and the first fragment I read dismayed me—a dialogue between the principal and this Felicity, concerning £50. I continued reading, but the work only declared the same conspiracy and fraud. I threw it aside and fled, but I soon returned, as if I was compelled to enjoy a self-flagellation.

What can I say about my first reading of those journals—a cavalcade of amusing connivance, two friends ripping up the world and making a fool of it— yet the disappointment of the 1910 journal was nothing compared to the violence I received from the last pages of the later journal, written days before Catherine's passing.

And so, in place of my dreams I have produced a true story that does not end well for anyone. I understand it was not entirely their fault—the connivance of a willing world is ever-present—but Catherine's words allow me no manoeuvring.

I cannot tell you how much this thing has taken out of me, for my endeavours have disinterred something monstrous hiding amongst the shadows of my being, which mocks my lost springs, and makes sport with my life's work. My nights became inhabited by strange dreams, fragmented narratives so worrisome and ugly they could only be evidence of neurosis or evil.

My heroine's little sins are easily understood and forgivable, but it's the endings which are so bad ... a rebuttal of all I hold sacred.

My hagiography was in ruins. Great Aunt Catherine's problematic place within the family memory, explained.

My publisher has requested I expunge from the text my traumas, including this Apologia and the projected last chapter. He advises me to make it a romantic comedy, but the world too often celebrates lies as if there is no alternative.

Great-aunt Catherine's work over one tumultuous year is attested by a series of articles dealing with woman's issues on the continent and published in a national newspaper, the *Daily Mail,*. To use them would be abetting a fraud.

The only crucial source is her 1910 journal, without which we would have a completely different story. I might use a few pages from the last journal, though *how* is a problem yet to be faced. I will decide when I get nearer to our brutal denouement.

You might think the conversations I record are my creations, but I can assure you, my integrity is beyond reproach. I do not embellish Catherine's words, which are often picturesque—the description of the Contessa is an example, while the Villa Vasari seems like Catherine's happy romance. Felicity as *butterfly* is Catherine's word, explaining Felicity shared with that creature its ability to re-create itself by metamorphosis and to display itself spectacularly, as well as its deceptively erratic flight. The Easter encounter at the Dewhirst family lunch is Catherine's record, wherein she does not fail to make herself one of the comedians.

If my narrative strikes you as staccato, it is because I have not invented. I do not add anything. At all times I'm indebted to her for the sense of any interpolation.

Some of her descriptions, especially about time or weather, I have cut up and applied them where they will add to the narrative flow, though it is hard to miss a peculiarity of mind which I have not manufactured.

My editor has chided me for lapsing into present tense, however I have faith the reader will understand the journal is not all smooth terrain, and where her text is sparse, I resort to conveying information briefly. I cite the last part of my Chapter 9. There, my passage mirrors the jotting in the journal which, we might suspect, Catherine's neglect of her journal is symptomatic of her neglect of Felicity.

More serious is my publisher's reaction to a word that persists in the many drafts. After explaining myself he put forward his objections, saying the character passes through the story like a ghost in various forms, which will be difficult for a reader to make a connection … and given the importance I have for the character, as one of only two heroes in the story, I should be less obscure and change the word. I concede his arguments, but I won't change the word. But I will clarify by citing John 15:13 and sometimes the terrible price of love.

By research I have attempted to introduce both women in Chapter 2's obituaries, and if you learn more about one than the other, then it's just how the facts are piled.

Felicity remains a little shaded, save for the testimony of Catherine, and, I am aggrieved to write, from a witness in the second journal, Pamela. A painful revulsion causes me to leave the fleeting Maud to the reader's insight.

The scattered remains of my heroine's lives are mapped out for you in the following few pages. They are now far beyond any horizon we are familiar with, but in their day they came together in friendship and love, and like two ships lit up in the black night, they glanced at each other in their passing and sailed on, never to forget their time. I know each recalled the other in their final moments.

I have stood before Felicity's grave and felt something strange from those gently smiling red roses growing wild there. Where Catherine stood in the 1960s, when she, seared by loss, bent by a reaction I do not have a name for, but which sprang from regret, and the realisation of her emotional failure … she was told the truth and that was the last burden she was to bear.

As it says in scripture, *Let the children come to me, and do not hinder them, for to such belongs the kingdom of God* …

The Truth about Catherine and Felicity and their year of 1910

Chapter 2.
Obit: Felicity, Catherine

Researching Felicity's background is like looking at a subject through the wrong end of a telescope. Traces of her life appear in the public record, and only occasional information about her background is offered in Catherine's journals.

Felicity came into this world in 1892, and left in 1947 after a painful illness.

Her family name is registered as Stanhope, but appears more administrative than real.

Latterly, she is known as Mrs Felicity Somersby, though she was never married, and was domiciled in the Somersby family seat, Manor Castlecrag, until her passing. The manor is extant and run as a youth hostel. She lived there from 1911, when she was not abroad, and is buried there.

Felicity made the Somersby seat something of a salon for the regional arts community, with a yearly festival and exhibition of works. You will hear her friend Pamela describing the usurpation of these festivities by a mayoral group, about which Felicity couldn't give a damn—a telling sketch of the fatalistic qualities taught to her by experience.

Felicity provided the world with two children who Catherine meets briefly in our story—more of this much later.

Other sources, which I have a reticence about revealing now, provide incontestable facts of her physicality.

As a young woman she stood 5 feet, 8 inches, with blonde hair always finely arranged, staring green eyes, skin *candidissimo,* and a figure both lithe and well-proportioned. Her physiognomy possessed a faun's alertness, with all her features sculpted to portray inquisitiveness and a readiness to flee.

Of her antecedents, this is what I discovered—her father was not her father, while her mother ran away when she was ten. Shortly after her mother's flight, Felicity was abandoned to an orphanage, never again to see her parents. Catherine records while in the orphanage another girl dragged Felicity into a stairwell and kissed her. The girl, whose name she could not remember, would pursue Felicity through several years and drag her away at strategic times until her dismay gave way to a flood of secret kisses, as if a desert was being quenched by a downpour.

On attaining adulthood, age 14, with only a rudimentary capacity to read or write, Felicity was let out for domestic service until her prettiness and genial disposition was noticed, whence she was given employment in a millinery shop, selling hats. This was advancement and an education too, as her clients were elegant women of a certain class who she learnt from, developing her own social performance. Catherine writes of her friend's fastidious grooming of her person, and of her social performance as a colourful butterfly's crazy flight.

Felicity became acquainted with the higher echelons of the London fine arts community, becoming a model and bagatelle of that oeuvre.

Her conceit was she served art; perhaps a substitute for her lack of religious belief. She was generous, flippant, and resigned, which put her at odds with her world, like our own, which always and forever understands self-interest. She was accepting of fortune's arrows and undemanding of love. I understand Catherine was the only object of her desire; however, there is one whose loss took her to the abyss … and another she repaid by rescuing from degradation and squalor … but neither is part of the year of our story.

You might find one episode quite a chilling display of a stoic character, as if she felt she deserved nothing much of life. I will let you make this discovery yourself. It seems to me she made good use of the energy she was born with and, like the physician's credo, she did no harm.

If you stay the course you will see her brought low by the one she loved. Then, in desperation, she reached out and sought refuge as a cleaner … and thence became a builder, and a promoter of her regional arts community. Quite an extraordinary life.

Whereas the familial influences of Felicity's antecedents are obscure, we know a great deal about where Catherine comes from. In fact, all we have to do to see our other heroine is to place our eye firmly to the telescope and all is revealed.

The Dewhirsts were an English family of landed gentry with roots deep into the northern sod. They emerged out of the political muck centuries before by getting lucky by choosing the winning side when the crown of England was at stake, but, lacking any kind of ambition or skill, almost immediately began a decline. A tiresome decline through a succession of litigious, brutish squires whose only recorded history was of public brawls, law suits with neighbours, and divorce proceedings. It was said the squires Dewhirst had more children under the thatched roofs of their tenants than behind the battlements of the manor house.

Catherine's great-granduncle, Sir George, had been kicked to death by his own horse, Hero. This enigmatic tragedy delivered the family stewardship to a sober younger brother who immediately rationalised the family assets.

The new patriarch was a prig with a vision. He replaced the large manor house with an eight-bedroom villa in Gothic Revival ecclesiastic style. The still extensive parklands were given back to farming and, as if the family blood sensed farming is a pastime best left to the sensible, these new lands were settled with rent-paying yeomen. The family's significant amount of idle time, previously dedicated to drinking, gambling, and the venting of spleen, was an obvious danger to the relaunched family, thus the new vision sought an occupation requiring little natural talent, and would also be an impediment to backsliding. Ergo, the eldest son was packed off to the Anglican seminary, and a new family tradition of social conformity begun.

By 1910, Catherine stood at the apogee of this redemptive story. At balls, Catherine would sit with the strong ladies with whom she could match polite wits. She also invested time with the less accomplished ladies and gave pleasure by her attention. Catherine would breeze through the dances, not bothering to dance well, was familiar with the servants, and involved in any naughtiness but made sure she was never caught. She was intelligent, diplomatic, insouciant, and was not a snob, but with a strong survival instinct. Her role as the daughter was to marry well—and if you saw her at a ball and knew what was going on, you might observe, 'Now, there's a girl who will marry whomever she wishes.' She made friends and admiring enemies easily, but through every change in life left them behind with an indelible memory of her dynamic self.

This picturesque sketch is meant to prepare the reader for a gloom that attended Catherine's father, the Reverend Harold Dewhirst, as if he sensed the *largeness of life*—which had been the curse of the family line and for a time had been stilled—may have resurfaced in his eldest child.

Reverend Dewhirst was no match for her. During their interlocutions, when the mace of Catherine's cosmopolitanism was battering the Reverend's disintegrating shield of orthodoxy, Mrs Agnes Dewhirst would ride to the rescue and tell her daughter to behave. Catherine's game was to keep the Reverend talking, not battering so well as to let this happen, because she needed him on the field of battle to satisfy her daughterly cruelty.

Mrs Agnes Dewhirst was something of a seer, predicting a European war against the Germans and calamity for her daughter—unlike the Reverend, who preached the horse would be extinct in ten years and life was to get better and better—and when the *calamity* came to pass, whilst the Reverend blustered with ineffectual outrage, Mrs Dewhirst was unsurprised and performed a series of variations on 'I told you so' which would have flattered J.S. Bach.

Catherine rode to hounds and competed with the leaders. She played golf and tennis with talent but not passion, and she wanted for nothing. And, if you forgive my indelicacy, the world was her oyster.

Looking at her portrait, a viewer would first notice her bountiful hair, a deep mass of brown waves seeming to defy discipline, which, as noted by more than one source, meant she and her hair were locked in a constant negotiation. I can also imagine a struggle between artist/ photographer and subject, and a capture or betrayal of a subtle impatience in the sitter, as if she were intolerant of the examination. Her eyes abide in recorded memory as a lively brown offering a sheltering calm and sympathy which was hard to resist. She was tall, not weighty or thin, but with what one might describe as athletic power, with not one ounce of her body mass given to anything other than an assured movement ruled by her will. She was an economy of force, like a golf swing; an elegance of controlled power. She was a Spartan maid, imagined by some high-minded aesthete.

Oh, paradoxical world! That a thoroughbred would consent to wear a bridle and be led by the likes of a Miss Felicity!

Chapter 3.
Felicity sells Catherine a hat

Miss Catherine Dewhirst, age twenty, recently down from the northern districts, newly resident in London and enrolled in a college of higher learning, wanted a new winter hat.

Catherine was not profligate in her expenditures. She'd tried the economising her father had encouraged her to be ruled by, but found it tired her. She decided a new purchase was needed to take her mind off the 'iron gates of life'—a line of poetry from her literature course which had convinced Catherine that buying a new winter hat was a reasonable riposte.

I invite you to see her as she promenades down Oxford Street, London in the early months of 1910, enjoying freedom from study in spite of the overcast, bitingly cold and windy winter's day.

What would her father, Reverend Harold Dewhirst, think, if he could see her breezing down Oxford Street, in pursuit of a new winter hat.

He may have exclaimed, 'I knew it!' … as if he'd imagined Viking marauders wading ashore, advancing upon his minor god-fearing town, driven forward by bulging codpieces, and threatening to sweep away faith, thrift and progress. If it was the 9th century he would be astride the fastest horse…but now, because of progress, the Reverend would be lamenting his capitulation to his daughter's pleas for a higher education—even though he knew, somehow, somehow he just knew, she was not really interested in a higher anything.

Miss Catherine Dewhirst did not believe in the horrors imagined by her much loved but unrevered father. Most often she was absorbed with getting what she wanted, and this day she wanted a new hat, which would also, momentarily, contradict her father's insistence on an imperfect world.

And so Miss Catherine Dewhirst is promenading down Oxford Street, finds the shop she has been recommended, opens the door and steps in, accompanied by a gust of cold air. Customers and staff turn and gaze censoriously at Catherine and her cold, invisible companion.

Miss Felicity comes in from the stock room carrying merchandise, sees Catherine bristling with indignation— her usual counter-offensive against injustice. Felicity sees her glowering eyes, and massed brown hair, and indicates to the new customer to approach the counter.

Felicity is a valued employee as she doesn't flirt with the gentlemen, is attentive to the ladies, and knows how to sell.

As Catherine begins explaining her millinery desires, Felicity interrupts with, 'Let me show you something, Miss. Please wait,' and she retreats to the storeroom to find a hat she has hidden.

Returning, she finds Catherine being served by her manager, who dismisses Felicity. Felicity, looking hopefully into Catherine's eyes, asks genteelly, 'Who do you wish serving you, Miss?'

For a moment a crisis is suspended before these three, but is resolved with a hesitant, 'Well, I did see you first.' The resolution of this drama has the manager politely withdrawing, and Felicity starts her selling.

'I have been saving this … for the right person, Miss,' and she offers the hat, an elegant variation on a British naval cap with a band spelling in antique gold lettering HMS *Britannia*. As Catherine styled the hat, other heads turned to watch the young woman as she gazed, fascinated, at her mirror image.

'Sown by Hanoverian peasants, Miss. The lining's velvet and the outer, Australian wool. One of our colonies, Miss. And the band, stitched by Yorkshire maidens. Very patriotic, Miss.'

Gazing into the mirror and serenaded by Felicity, Catherine was pleased, 'How much …'

'Only two pounds, five shillings, Miss. All quality, you can see by the velvet lining. And the tassels are black silk. See? I attached them myself. Look, stitched as a British crown, Miss.'

Catherine was aghast at the price, but Felicity's merchandising was up to the challenge. 'Let me ask my manager, Miss.' Felicity and the manager spoke at length, one speaking, then the other, back and forth it was until they agreed they should take lunch at The Pepper Pot, where Felicity remarked of a waiter who seemed very attentive to her manager, to which her manager replied, 'Surely, I don't know what you mean.'

Catherine, ensorcelled by her mirror image, was interrupted by, 'Two pounds, Miss.'

'Two pounds! Then I will starve for weeks.'

'Then starve, Miss. On you it's positively violent. Take the hat at one pound, eighteen shillings. It's made to keep you warm, Miss, and to shelter your beautiful brown hair from the filthy fog.'

As Catherine Dewhirst decided on the hat, the room resumed its attention to its own concerns.

They moved to the wrapping table, where Catherine stood over Felicity, looking down at her exquisitely knitted blonde hair, watching two of the most beautiful hands she had ever seen wrap her parcel with a finesse she found strangely moving. Catherine felt an impulse to both compliment this person and thank her for her service, but chose a masquerade and remarked how interesting was the bracelet on Felicity's wrist—the band being three interlaced flat ropes of gold, with two birds at the clasp, their bodies precious gems, while their heads rested on their bodies as if together asleep.

'Do you like it, Miss? I know it will look wonderful on you,' and Felicity took off the bracelet and whisked it into the parcel, whispering, 'I'm a valued employee, but I can still get into trouble. That will be one pound, eighteen shillings, Miss.'

Catherine's surprise was about to say something, but instead offered the purchase price. As Felicity wrote out the docket, 'Do you know the Chop Shop? I worry about you starving, Miss. They have good food at a good price. I take my meal there at seven. You can give the bracelet back if it doesn't suit … but I can tell it does.' Catherine, while trying to find something in Felicity's eyes, took the parcel, they exchanged pleasantries as befitted a lady and a serving girl, and so our heroines met.

It was several days before Catherine summoned the courage to attend the Chop Shop, and it did look respectable, though the clientele grew more dubious as the evening matured, when it filled with the residue of the closing local entertainments, with toffs and their escorts who were not their wives, and fancy young men who were attentive to the unescorted ladies.

Felicity was sitting with a group of models and artists' assistants—the latter were young men who mixed the paints and prepared the canvases or painted what the artist could get away with not doing themselves—when she saw Catherine's hesitant entrance.

'You've come, Miss!'

'Well, I have to return your beautiful bracelet.'

'Keep it, Miss. I knew it would suit you,' and Felicity took the bracelet out of Catherine's hand and wrapped it around her wrist. 'You see, it has finally come home. A great lady gave it to me. She begged me not to run away and marry her son. But I said I had no intension of marrying. She was so grateful … she took off that bracelet right in front of me and insisted I take it. What could I do? To refuse would have said her son was worthless, which he wasn't. He was just a prisoner of his family. So

I accepted. She was so happy … and so was I, as I am now. Why spoil that?'

'What a curious story. But how can I wear it, knowing this history?'

'What history? It's gold. No one throws gold away. They reuse it. Why … this gold may have been given by Solomon to the Queen of Sheba. Now it adorns your wrist. And if I had my choice to have dinner with you or the Queen of Sheba, then I would choose … I would choose you, Miss.'

'You are quite a saleswoman … even when you are giving something away. I am Catherine, Catherine Dewhirst, from Durham. And you?'

'Felicity, Miss Catherine … from nowhere,' and Felicity laughed stupidly and continued with a voice reverberating with self-consciousness, 'I can hear the cannon balls striking the walls of your penetrable castle. Come, Cathy, let's go and find some interesting food,' and Felicity grabbed Catherine's hand and towed her out of the public house into the darkened street, as if she were her prize, as if her prize was the Temeraire.

They climbed into a hansom cab, Felicity bantering with the driver, then collapsing into a corner of the cabin, from where she stared at her companion, who sat forward, apprehensive of the unknown. Catherine wondered if the horse also listened to the glorious clip-clop of its shoes on the street stones as the passing streetlight filtered in as a cascade of ephemeral revelations of a reclining Felicity, her eyes soft and fixed upon her Catherine, and then she spoke: 'Miss Catherine Dewhirst of Durham. You are the most beautiful girl I will ever see.'

The London of 1910 was a product of the rampant commercialisation which was the Victorian era. Though poverty was rife, and class barriers were a highly functioning reality, society experienced a lessening of its strictures, especially around the edges, where the classes met. It would have been unusual for a high-end shopgirl to befriend a lady, but the fact they were young allowed our heroines to form an alliance against the norm.

Perhaps it was just the vulnerability of youth to romance that brought them together and allowed these friends to ignore the standards of their day. No analysis appears in Catherine's journal, so it's my imagination that has one leading the other by the hand and imploring her, as a child pleads with its mother, while the other acts the patrician and enjoys the game of the other dying for love of her. Their sin of wilfulness seems evident to me, but hardly accounts for their fall; that is clearly due to the concupiscence of those diverse and perennial types who seek to gain by the fortune or ruin of others.

Felicity called the cab to stop, paid the driver, and pulled her friend into the night.

'Cathy, do you want to see me?' and without waiting Felicity pulled her new friend across the street, into a public house which was the preserve of men.

Through the doors they went at speed, past the dozy drinkers, and up the stairs and into another room one might describe as a club, and before the *concierge* could recover from his amazement at seeing women in this place, Miss Felicity pointed to the painting above the bar and announced, 'Look, Cathy, it's me, your Felicity.'

Catherine looked at the painting of a naked opalescent girl holding an earthenware jar on her shoulder, in what was an irrelevant oriental harem setting.

A controversy was rising, and Catherine felt a tug and they were careering out of the club. Speed had delivered them to the street without a hurt, and they hurriedly walked on, until Felicity found the café and they were shown to a table.

They sat with silence until, 'Are you a courtesan?' and Felicity looked at her love but could not stop bursting into laughter. It was like a music hall joke which was funny because it was wrong and predictable.

'No, my darling, I'm just an artist's model. Though sometimes my work is for art, and sometimes, as you have seen, less artistic.'

'You mean … you take your clothes off, to be painted, for money.'

Felicity felt as if a dozen words had been demanded of her to describe something that needed much conversation. Then Catherine rose and walked out of the café.

◆ ◆ ◆

The following days were terrible for both our heroines. Felicity's grief weighed on her personality, smothering her natural warmth so barely a spark escaped to comfort a suffering world. Being this morose made her feel like a drudge, far below the noble free, but what course was open to her except to snare a man, the richer the better, and to become his servant? Still, her friend's rejection was a correct thing too, correct according to their stations, and she must mourn, be unhappy, get through the coming weeks, and go on.

For Catherine it was far worse. She was not use to failure. Her nerves, usually so calm, seemed in open rebellion, as if she were a piano being sawn in half, reverberations exploding through her body that no thought could placate. She made herself go for a walk, only to find her tortured nerves accompanied her. As the days passed, her nerves grew more intense until she was compelled to resolve whatever was persecuting her.

'Felicity,' a voice whispered through the icy darkness, and Felicity saw a figure standing like a beggar under a streetlamp's sick yellow, and she called to her friends she would catch them up. 'Catherine, is it you? How long have you been here?'

'I thought you closed at six o'clock.'

'No, we were counting stock. You must be freezing. Oh my! Your hands are ice!'

'I just wanted to tell you … I'm sorry.'

'No, it was my fault. I wanted you to see me as more than a shop girl. But we must get you warm.'

They went into the first warm place they found, a high-end restaurant waiting for its evening diners with a maître-d' from whom Felicity ordered a hot soup entrée.

The soup arrived with a plate of steaming hot towels. Felicity placed a towel on each of her friend's hands and reached under Catherine's dress to place two towels on her ice-cold knees.

'I'm in the National Gallery. In a Burne-Jones painting. He used me for a character to balance a drawing of one of his lady friends. I think I was too fair … not really his type … but I'm there. Cathy, have you seen how the poor and weak are treated in our land? Surely you cannot hate me for serving art, and standing as far away from poverty as I can be, even though art is for the rich?'

'I liked seeing your painting. I don't understand how a shopgirl can give me a gold bracelet. I don't know how the beautiful words I'm studying will help me write banal ones about flower shows and debutant balls.'

'Then you are worried about the future. The future is too big to be worried about. Let me be your little future, and cast me aside when you've had enough.'

'You see, even you sound brutal. You, who have been kind and generous to me.'

'Cathy, our waiter sent us hot towels because he saw you were cold. That is not to be expected in a place like this. But I have exciting news ... I've joined a suffragette chapter. I am a suffragette!'

Catherine was included in all of Felicity's socialising, which included soirées given by the owners of her millinery shop—the conversation being almost entirely about advantage and gossip, and occasional observation of our heroines' companionship.

Chapter 4.
Spring, Highgate Cemetery

The end days of March 1910 in London saw the exhausted generals of winter decamp to southern worlds, to marshal their resources for a renewed campaign in the north nine months hence, taking with them their violent howl and the other severe instruments of their season, but leaving behind an expendable rearguard of fanatics to resist the hated spring until the end. Over the roofs of London, down its narrow streets, and through its bare patient trees, the winter rearguard fought on with a diminishing malevolence. One could tell by the jaunty step of the well-to-do, and a kind light in the eyes of the poor, something optimistic and irresistible was advancing at the ebbing of winter's sorrows.

The cold still wrapped around the London living but now only penetrated to human warmth by careless invitation—an undone button, a hatless head or gloveless hand. From horizon to horizon the London sky was a subfusc curd, as if the last of winter could only impose this sombre vault, a mirror to the River Thames. It was under this grim last stand our heroines sought to celebrate their antipodeanism in Highgate Cemetery, by viewing the fantastical Egyptian Road.

The omnibus dropped the friends at the cemetery's main entrance, a neo-Gothic building with features squeezed unsettlingly into the coffinesque façade, a telling presentiment, as when the curtain first rises at the theatre.

'Why this frozen welcome? Is it trying to scare us, do you think?' Catherine exhumed something from her years attending her father 'Dear Pater might declare 'narrow is the gate' for the redeemed, somewhere in Matthew I think … which is supposed to be both warning and give hope. Kit, hold my hand if that brick beast scares you.'

'I will, Cat. Then you cannot leave me behind if that horror metamorphoses into a mean old reaper, and chases us for being too gay. I'm told such phenomena often happened in the ancient world.'

Hand in hand they walked the descending way toward the Egyptian Road, sharing a morbid flippancy while taking in the sombre architectural grandeur of the tombs which offered no entry for the living or exit for the interred.

Catherine remarked the pathos of forgotten remembrances … so much of living was waiting for something to happen, but here, it was probably best nothing happens.

They walked through Highgate Cemetery on a cold March Sunday afternoon, and finding the place she sought, Felicity pulled her friend into a nave, unseen from the pathway.

'Cathy, close your eyes, my darling,' and as Catherine closed her eyes, Felicity rose up on her toes, put her arms around her friend's waist and kissed her passionately on her warm soft lips, and then all about her face, and as Catherine responded by turning her friend so she had laid her against the wall, and as her arms lifted her dress her waist moved softly against her friend, and Catherine heard her love transported—'My dear, dear friend. I love, I love, I love you'—and Catherine opened her eyes and saw her beloved transfigured by that distant bell, that she'd never seen before, a ringing she had only experienced in the privacy of her own bed, and as the crisis rose, peaked, and washed over them, Catherine heard a whispered ecstatic cry of 'Will you marry me, Cathy Dewhirst? Will you wait with me for something to happen?'

As the tide of pleasure slowly abated and the mystery they shared was dissipating, Felicity heard, 'Of course not, you silly thing.'

Chapter 5.
Easter holiday with the Dewhirst family

Spring appeared in London as a shy tentative innocent, as if it couldn't remember kicking to death the rearguard of winter and stomping its remains through a stormwater grate. The glory of the Easter ritual and holiday followed on as a great victory is followed by a great celebration, and Catherine invited Felicity home for the holiday. They would take the afternoon train and arrive late. Then a midnight horse-drawn cab ride to The Grange.

In the morning Felicity was piqued to find Catherine gone—she had left for the hunt. Felicity descended to the dining room and was greeted by a table stacked with breakfast delights. There was Mrs Dewhirst, who remarked what a beautiful girl she was, and the servant Annie, intent on being the best servant she could be, and there was Catherine's sixteen-year-old brother, Algernon, already ensorcelled by the guest.

Felicity noticed the bounty and the boy at the same time and thought, how delicious. She moved toward the table and used bird looks to express to the young gentleman he should hold the chair for her so she would be seated correctly. And in the same language she made it clear to the young gentleman his intervention had made her seating—her correct approximation to the banquet arranged for her pleasure and sustenance—successful by his most excellent efforts. In fact, she remarked, breaking into the human tongue, if not for his kindnesses, in attempting to sit she might have missed the chair completely. And it would have been obvious what the consequences would have been—her warm and yielding posterior would have collided with the cold and unyielding floor to produce a sensation …

By then Algy had lost his following of her sentences, the entire tract reduced to a few gilt words uttered by a beautiful immortal descended from London, and stored in his heart forever.

Felicity thus became acquainted with Master Algernon Dewhirst, the next candidate for the Anglican seminary.

Algy was so smitten he told his bestest friend Messalina, a town girl, in prolonged detail of his infatuation and received a most violent push which sat him on his bottom and left him thinking she'd never done that before!

Riding boots upon the parquet floor has Felicity leaning around the wing of a high-backed couch to pixy, 'Hi ho, Cathy! Algy's been telling me the family secrets. Surely they can't all be true! There's a Charles Broadmoor in the library … seems ever so eager to see you. You must tell me all about him.'

And Felicity called to a disappearing Catherine, 'Algy is going to name one of his chickens after me … we're going now to see the pretty thing. Algy … as much as I love your sister, she doesn't have a sense of, dramatic tension. Lead me to your coop, my hero.'

◆ ◆ ◆

The lunch began with bowed heads as the Reverend delivered a prayer. Having finished his sacred duty the Reverend fired the first genial salvo, asking Felicity about her *antecedents*. If you remember Felicity's obituary, you might suspect *antecedences* might be a subject to inspire an enigmatic reply, coloured by her long abandonment in the orphanage.

'Pray, Miss Felicity, where do your parents hail from?'

'Hail from, Reverend? That is the least of my parental concerns. I should very much like to know where they are now. Or should I say, I would like to know where *any* of them are. Surely they would be up to no good.'

The Reverend was perplexed. He was stuck on a little word he just could not hurdle, so resumed with, 'Pardon me, but what does *any* signify?'

Catherine interposed with, 'Felicity is in demand in the London art scene, as a model. Knows all the famous painters. She's even in the National Gallery. Isn't that right, Kit.'

'That is correct. Let me demonstrate' and Felicity stood and struck an artistic pose. 'I can do this for hours. It's a talent.'

Algy exploded with applause, 'Wonderful! I can barely sit still in class.'

Charles: 'Will you give us an insight in the London art scene?' to which Felicity replied, 'Yes, I can, Charles. Augustus John is an idiot.'

The Reverend said he didn't know that gentleman, while Charles giggled, and Algy was beside himself with an enthusiastic, 'Of course, it's true.'

The Reverend tried the national debt, international politics, and even St Paul's letters to the Romans, about which he was ready to launch a fascinating declamation which was not without controversy, but somehow these topics never seemed to ignite the lunchtime sensibility.

Rather, Felicity and her *energies* reigned in tandem with Mrs Dewhirst's banquet, the former being a little bit odd and the latter a more heightened culinary experience than the norm.

Felicity: 'Do you know, Cat, while you were chasing around the countryside after poor, innocent Mr Fox, Mr Fox was here, in this very house, in this very room, playing Old Maid with the Reverend and me. It's true! Mr Fox would look up from his cards, held in those cute little paws, and gaze out the window, listening to the distant thundering hooves and trumpet calls. And he'd sadly shake his little, pointy red furry face, in a most disapproving way. We played twelve games, and the Reverend was the Old Maid twelve times!'

'What a losing streak!' Algy exclaimed.

'I hear you are thinking of entering parliament, Charles,' the slightly distracted Reverend asked, as if he couldn't remember playing cards with Mr Fox.

'Yes. I've been offered a place, and I'm thinking it through.'

Catherine's fascination with this sensible dialogue was interrupted by Felicity.

'But we, Algy and I, have some even more important news. We are engaged to be married. The dear boy asked me at the chicken coop and—well, I didn't have to think. And let me thank Mrs Dewhirst for this wonderful luncheon.'

Algy managed a surprised, 'What an idea! Simply grand. Father, this means I won't have time to go to the seminary.'

'You can practise medicine instead,' Felicity chirruped, as if hitting a shuttlecock for a winner. 'And I will be your first patient, though I can assure you, I am in the best of health. People often remark on my health. It must be another talent. The hobbling masses will flock to you, Algy … or … they will hobble to you, in a flock.'

Catherine offered a studied, 'But Felicity, dear, Algy is only sixteen years old, and there are laws governing such things. Which your … impulsive behaviour seems to ignore, and—'

'It's true, Cat. I'm not premeditated. Spain! We'll move to Spain. People can marry in Spain if they throw a stone through a church window. It's one of those quaint customs one finds in foreign lands that defy reason … probably due to too much sun and wine. And anyone can marry anyone in Spain. Perhaps Cat, we can go there too. It's a wonderful, sensible land. And Algy, we can sleep to the middle of the day, you can cure the sick in the afternoon, then we can dance through the night. And you can bring the hen known as Felicity. We will need eggs.'

Algy added gravely, 'Grand, simply grand. I must tell Messalina.'

Then the luncheon seemed to lose any recognisable form, a startled Felicity asking who was Messalina, and if she were pretty; the Reverend saying something about the seminary while appealing with his eyes to Mrs Dewhirst, who was letting the unimportant things evaporate. Charles was congratulating the betrothed, while Algy was confessing in an animated way about studying medicine, and to restore order Catherine was insisting Felicity help her in the kitchen.

On their return Felicity was very quiet and Catherine took responsibility for the table talk, which relaxed into a more sedate mien—the better to assist digestion—about people who'd been met recently and others who hadn't, and the Reverend enquiring after Mr Broadmoor's prospective career, and Mr Broadmoor enquiring after Catherine's studies in London, and Algy searching his own life for whatever might entertain Felicity, while Mrs Dewhirst made sure everyone was provided for.

It was when the last spoonful of brandy-soaked trifle was being shovelled home that Felicity, like an anthropomorphic volcano having held its peace a moment longer than was possible, genteelly erupted, apropos of nothing, with 'I have dined in Devonshire House', which stopped everyone in whatever they were doing. The ensuing silence, whether they wished it or not, seemed to beg the speaker to continue.

'I was asked to accompany a gentleman who needed a partner for the evening. I received a dress out of it, because I had to look the part, though Lord knows on what occasion I can wear *that* dress again. He was very nice. I wore his family jewellery. Absolutely beautiful … he remarked I was a little numinous. The house is bigger than a metropolitan Town Hall … you could put a museum inside. And the staircase! It was like walking on clouds up to heaven. The talk was fascinating. I'd been warned it could be political … that I shouldn't listen. Another gentleman, a government minister I think, escorted us into the library for coffee. He told an amusing story about General Buller, commander of our forces against the Boer. It seems the General was so attached to Lady Londonderry he would write letters telling her the details of his planned offensives … via the postal service!'

It was Algy who broke the silence by exploding with laughter and exclaiming, 'HA HA! WHAT AN EGG! HURRAH FOR MISS FELICITY!'

'Algy! Don't be vulgar,' Mrs Dewhirst gently scolded.

◆ ◆ ◆

The following day Felicity was to meet her future common-law husband.

While Charles had reluctantly returned to his family and prospective constituent, and Algy was consorting with Messalina, Catherine and Felicity decided to walk into town, across pleasant green fields teased by a kindly drizzle.

Outside a tavern Lord Clarence Somersby sat taking lunch. This person was a landed aristocrat whose antecedents occupied more than a page in Debrett's. He had been born so wealthy it would be difficult for him not to die in that blessed state. However, there was to be a war, a depression, another war, and then taxes, which put an end to where his money came from. He was a patron of the arts and a collector, his enthusiasm being medieval works, especially Italian—though for some reason he had no interest in icons or chubby baby Jesuses. He avoided Northern Europe as men avoid venereal decease (his joke) and spent his time lounging around the Mediterranean pond, only returning to manage his business affairs and replenish those few things of British manufacture he desired. He thought it only fair the Somersby bones should have rest from the usual brave service to monarch and state.

Felicity approached and asked if he remembered her, an occasion a year earlier at a Burne-Jones retrospective …

Yes, of course, and Felicity asked him if he was satisfied with it and he answered thoughtfully, 'That is a question. That … is a question. I own two of his pictures … but I have to separate them from my Fra Angelicos and the old masters. Those are in my gallery … while the Joneses are about the house, filling the walls. I don't know what that says. It's not fair to either, but if I had to say … I would say, it's not fair. Perhaps they are two different types of imagining. I would be more confident in saying … your friend here, wouldn't have to push her way into a Jones picture.'

'Yes. He would call her a stunner,' and Felicity grabbed hold of Catherine's bountiful brown hair, and with her beautiful fingers draped the lot to one side, revealing her friend's bare neck and soft cheek and an exquisitely sculpted ear, and Lord Somersby laughed with delight at the transformation while Catherine blushed and Felicity beamed proudly at her friend.

'I wonder,' continued Felicity, 'if we might call in, to view your collection? We are leaving Tuesday for London, but we could leave early, and arrive late, if we called in. I wonder if you would be agreeable to visitors, Lord Somersby?'

'Well, my dear, my house is … it is an object of neglect. My own fault for staying where I like better. I would be embarrassed to entertain, and I'm sorry for putting my flaws before your pleasant society.'

But Felicity acted the seer. 'Beware Sir, Catherine is the apple of her father's eye. And her father is the unstable Vicar Dewhirst of Durham Cathedral. A firebrand, a follower of John Ball, and nothing more inspires him to vengeance than a slight to his favourite. A most violent man, Sir, capable of raising the ignorant masses. If safe passage is now in the offing, you must not antagonise the natives … seize it, at whatever price. I see a barricaded highway, your motor car stopped. Pitchforks, clubs, burning torches. Oh, dear God! They will not be appeased with your fine words or pistols at twenty paces.'

Lord Somersby for a moment believed, then acquiesced with, 'I've met your Reverend Dewhirst several times, and a more correct parson I could not imagine. However, one can never tell, where a family slight might be felt… I'll have a carriage waiting at the station from ten o'clock Monday morning. I'll expect you to stay the night, and I'll get you to the next morning train to London.'

'Bravo, my lord. No special fare for us. We will live in anticipation of your collection,' Felicity declared as she was dragged away by Catherine, who called behind her, 'Please excuse my friend's high spirits. Art affects her,' to which Lord Somersby surprised himself by calling back, 'I'll look forward to your visit. We will see what comes of it.'

How can living be anything other than what it is, from an initial incapacity coupled to a growing rambunctious but dubious self-belief, then an inglorious descent or a dyspeptic sojourn back to infantilism, immobility, and death … an insect must have a more clear perspective of beginnings and ends! But between these, our poles, what are we doing but playing a role for the comfort of one's delusions ... but while we are going at it, in all our glitter, we do not know what fate awaits us around any corner, in any tomorrow, even from a neighbour's secret malice … or even in the tangles of one's own puny decision? Surely this chaos is meant to wreck our conceits and cast doubt on every belief!

As our heroines walked home, the day seemed to spin around, and its dour indolence metamorphosed into a spring display of new love, the fall of the breeze raising the temperature a degree or two. The sheeted cloud now broke up and became separated by ponds of blue, and the trees glistened aloud as great mounds of greenness veiled in mists of diamonds, a miracle made of fresh raindrops teased to laughter by happy sunshine. The blue of the sky drew the eye up to worship a moment truly pleasant, kind, and beautiful.

While Catherine complained to her friend she should be more decorous when speaking to the genteel of society, Felicity sang part of a French song and put one arm around her Cat's waist and said, 'I want to see his collection … but I want to see *the* collection more.

Felicity added, 'My dear, darling, love of my life … Lord Somersby has the most valuable collection of erotica in England.'

◆ ◆ ◆

I've already revealed that Felicity becomes entangled with Lord Somersby, which is another story beyond the frame of my tale, but the traits of this individual I will now launch myself upon as it might be of interest later. Though he is a passer-by in our story, my interest in his Lordship might help me in my promise to produce a 100-page novella, which, it seems, will be running a tidy bit short. As I've declared Catherine's journal to be my natural borders, this places upon me a welcome discipline I wish the great mass of our contemporary authors, who manufacture words as if they are satisfying an addiction, were also ruled by.

Anyway, it cannot hurt to know someone who spends a productive life with one of our heroines and stands in attendance, as a passive accomplice, at one of the bitter ends of this story.

He was a shy man, given to displaying an irritability which spoke of insecurity. He was not tall and his facial expression was demure, hesitant and plain, in spite of a pleasant symmetry of features. His natural demeanour was suspicious and bleak. Romances for him had been lined up in deep ranks by his own class, but after a tedious game without high points it was declared a nil-all draw and both sides retreated from the wasteland.

He was not many things, but he wasn't a fool or a clichéd type, like the buffer who disappears into his club's leather-bound chairs ... he didn't tell stories or hail fine fellows, nor did he attend places where these fellows could be hailed and regaled.

He only had confidence in a narrow stratum of life which he pursued through his traveling, studying, and collecting.

Without burdening you further, let me say simply this: they did not marry, they had two children, spent most of the year abroad, and he noticed his Italian friends were warmer in her company. Much of this comes from their son, as confided to Catherine and recorded in the final pages of her second journal.

The friends arrived by train at the nearest village, and travelled by donkey cart to the Manor Castlecrag, which was, as its owner confessed, run-down, and suffering from a lack of administration. The inglorious crowning of Manor Castlecrag was its roof, a frozen oscillation which should have worried any inhabitant, while the interior was gripped by the infirmities of a neglected old age. By a strange natural selection, the house servants seemed to have surrendered their vitality to their environment.

The guests walked through the house trying not to observe the breakdown of standards. Though the rooms prepared for them were of a higher standard, the guests decided to share one room, a decision met with relief by the servants.

The master appeared at two o'clock to escort his guests to luncheon, arranged, because the day was most fine, on a terrace overlooking the garden, now run to seed, but offering a distant landscape so pleasant to view Catherine remarked she hoped Lord Somersby would never own it—a row of heroic trees on the horizon, their canopy edging a breathtaking blue sky pinned by a few white woolly clouds drafted by a child.

The luncheon fare was inedible. Catherine made a point of eating nothing and took only tea and a biscuit. Felicity accused her host of ignorance, and hoped his collection was not to this standard, dropping her utensils with a clang to signify outrage.

A mortified host escorted his guests to the gallery—a classically decorated room with black walls hung with a fine collection of mediaeval art and old masters in gilt frames, and lit by skylights.

Felicity pointed to a Madonna and said she recognised the hand signal, and the host seemed to revive, 'Yes, that is so, and look here … a gesture indicating forgiveness.'

'Then we will take it as a sign and forgive you too,' Felicity said, and their host relaxed and in a soft cultured voice confessed his house was a mess. 'It reminds me of everything that makes me uncomfortable. It's a prison in a foreign land to me … more enemy than family. But I cannot discard it, so I flee … My cowardice is the neglect you experience'

'Perhaps,' Catherine began, 'it is not cowardice, but revenge.'

'Not a bad stab, Miss Dewhirst. You will live to be a wily, if unpopular, journalist.' And as this strangely prescient sentiment passed, Felicity saw a chance to reveal the delicate ambitions bringing them to Manor Castlecrag.

'May I enquire of your other collection? I have heard it described as an achievement in artistic sensibility.'

'Miss Felicity! I should have been more wary of you. I am shocked you know of it.'

'I model … and artists talk. Some think models have no brains or ears. My Cat and I are most interested in viewing your collection, for artistic reasons.'

'I don't show it. I cannot be accused of corrupting … so I have arranged for tea and cakes from the village in the orangery. And there's an end of it.'

Felicity was prepared for a contest, 'But it isn't corrupting, is it? Otherwise, you would be corrupt, is that not right?' and as the host was about to qualify, Felicity continued her reasoning 'It is art, isn't it … more sensual than usual, more explicit, perhaps. They are produced, aren't they? As I hear, some from societies different than ours? If these things are collected, then they should be seen. What is the danger in seeing?'

'"Should" is the word you use, Miss. "Might" is a better word for your argument, and I'm saying, that is my prerogative,' and in a flash both parties recognised the stumble. Felicity laughed and put her arm in her host's and exclaimed, 'I am looking forward to tea, and my friend is famished, aren't you, my dear Cat?'

Catherine's journal describes both women chipping away at their host's 'might.' Lord Somersby offered justifications, both moral and proprietorial, until carelessly playing the 'women's virtue' card.

The effect was a lightning bolt—the poor man saw his guests' posture straighten, their eyes, glacial. The host's dialogue trailed off as he watched Catherine put down her teacup, and as if addressing a stupid and wayward child, 'Lord Somersby … I have no idea what this collection is, but it seems more controversial than pattern work. I guess at least some of the subjects might be female, yes? So where is your concern for these women's virtue? It seems women can be the subject of your collection, included in its situations, even celebrated, but they cannot view these things they are part of. No answer is necessary, my lord, but a defence of your prejudices is as unacceptable as your ramshackle house.'

Felicity: 'Please, Cat, remember we are guests.'

As Lord Somersby looked inward at the face of hypocrisy, he might have seen a little of what was judged not right by his Mediterranean associates. Realising what had already been decided, he invited his guests to inspect a few of the more artistic artefacts.

Catherine describes the library where the collection was held:

Rosewood panels with a deep antique sheen. Fine classical detailing, Doric pilasters, with triglyphs, and metopes filled with bucrania in the frieze; an exotic fire-place surround of green, brown and yellow veined marble with nude Atlantes holding up a heavy entablature. Wicked Egyptian Revival chandelier with eight arms and glass bowls, winged sphinxes on the arms, dark drama. Glass cabinets, filled with erotic objects, phalli. Paintings and sculptures of nudes, figures in congress ... fascinating ...

Catherine would return to this room many decades hence, on a mission to possess one of its objects, only to find it stripped bare. As a consequence of the sojourn and recovery of the object, she would meet her end.

Lord Somersby began selecting his objects, but soon let his enthusiasm for the subject dictate his lesson.

There was Jupiter and Ganymede, cavorting satyrs, excited bacchantes, and deux amies dodues, celebrant les rites de Lesbos; Shaktis of Civa; Mars going at Venus; an impossibly balletic girl arched over backwards while satisfying with all her lips two gods from India; hermaphrodites; Persian miniatures of women and gentlemen, with another gentleman giving it to the first gentleman from the rear, in a healthy open-air setting; a prostrate Buddha-Siamese lady receiving attention from her gentleman; vases decorated with a variety of sexual positions and acts impossible, some impossible to be pleasurable; and a print of Jean-Baptiste II Lemoyne's *Loth et filles* had a peeking Catherine squeal, 'My God, is that what I have to accommodate on my wedding night?'

The showing was a success—the conversation became animated, the lord resuming his place as authority and genial host.

Our heroines caught the Tuesday morning train to London, seen on their way by Lord Somersby, who was inhabited by an unusual feeling, a gladness of heart, and who, on returning to his manor, was confounded by what he seemed to discover for the first time.

After a number of days, and the gradual re-familiarisation with the status quo, Lord Somersby returned to his post-lapsarian, pre-Felicitian state.

Chapter 6.
Suffragettes

I found this letter from Felicity folded into the journal. I have not trifled with the message other than to correct the many misspellings.

Precious Puss.

Everyone comments how happy I am but I just love selling hats and it's true. Listen I'm going to a suffragette march will you come and watch me. Please my love I want to scream for our rights and I know if you are there I will have the gift. Miss holding your hand miss your protection. Miss miss miss you. Place and time on back.

Forever Your Kit

DOWN WITH THE OPPRESSORS AND BURN THEIR HOUSES

The march to the Houses of Parliament was mustering behind a committee of a dozen firebrand females draped in furs and armed with offensive-looking walking sticks and, behind them 300 women from diverse social strata and a scattering of male supporters—this phalanx overflown by gently fluttering banners and placards standing to wobbly attention declaring for women's rights and the vote.

'Oh, most wonderful! I'm so glad!' exclaimed Felicity as her friend put her arm around her neck and kissed her.

'What you are doing here, Kit? These parades can get violet, and I've a dread something unexpected might happen.'

'Dear … dearest Cat, you are a peach for coming, and what a show you look. I knew that hat was only meant for you. Do you know we are oppressed? It's true! Do you know there has never been a female admiral in the British navy? Not one, not even a captain. And why not? Except for you … the captain of my heart.'

'Do you really want to go to sea? And who do you want to vote for?'

'Well … I don't know. But, look Cat, the noise, the crowd, and the signs. It's such exquisite fun. We scream our heads off in the street! And, look,' and Felicity opened her hand to reveal a potato, 'some of us decided to bring eggs or tomatoes, but I could only get this.'

The friends pondered the missile in Felicity's gentle though not quite innocent hand, but they did not hear their hearts thumping in their breasts, or the music of the spheres as it played up a storm, or the spud's telepathic pleading of 'take me back to the kitchen, dearie.'

'I'm going to knock a helmet off a policeman's head. Look at my sign. I made it myself.'

A hunting trumpet sounded and Felicity reached up and kissed her friend. 'Wish me luck, my love. Will you watch me? Stay where I can see you.'

And the parade was off, moving from Marble Arch in loose array down to Whitehall with the desultory slovenliness of a peasant army on the march, effusing the weird bonhomie of a riot in a mental institution, while the general public came out of their shops and parks to watch and partake in many little conversations for and against. Eventually they reached their furthest gain line, in a commercial area more than 300 yards from the Houses of Parliament, confronted by a line of policeman and mounted constabulary.

Equilibrium had been achieved by the precious no-man's-land separating the two forces. Slogans and taunting assaulted the police line, followed by speeches from suffragette luminaries and a sympathetic politician.

A few vegetables were also launched at the police. Felicity too had decided to launch her potato at the prominent hat of whiskered policeman.

Moving to the front ranks, and judging all variables were now at their optimum, Felicity launched her missile, but with more gusto than accuracy allowed … for it sailed over the head of the targeted policeman, the brief flight consummated by the potato smashing a neat hole through a large shopfront window, followed by the kind of thoughtful pause which usually follows the asking of a question. As the consequences could not be denied, the window collapsed with a mighty roar, drowning out the suffragette speaker, and eliciting an eerie and bipartisan silence.

As the last pieces of glass tinkled to the ground, the whiskered officer with the prominent hat drew out his whistle and blew. The police line moved forward, beating down resistance, pushing those who were not dispersing quickly enough. Cries and panicked exclamations filled the air. Suffragettes were brained; others fell and were trampled. Felicity was retreating, saying, 'Excuse me, excuse me please.'

Seeing Catherine across the street, she started in the direction of safety, but a strong hand seemed to have hold of her arm—the hand belonged to the high-hatted and whiskered policeman.

Felicity looked into steely eyes, at mutton-chop whiskers, as a mouth curled by cruelty said, 'You're coming with me, Missy.'

'I haven't done anything. It wasn't me. I'm meeting my friend,' and she called out, 'Cathy!' as she tried to pull away.

'I seen what you done. Come along now, girlie.'

Just as our heroine appeared lost, the policeman's duty was interrupted by a rap on his hat from an umbrella held by a large middle-aged lady, who offered several more raps as if beating time to her chant of 'Unhand-that-gal-Sir. How-dare-you-assault-a-lady.'

The policeman had his arrest well in hand until the umbrella caught him in the ribs, and an even more committed thrust to his stomach all but winded him, causing him to lose his grip on the girl.

As Felicity fled, the officer turned on the umbrella woman, batted away her weapon, picked her up and carried her to the police-wagon.

Catherine listened to an excited Felicity. 'Did you see that? They tried to arrest me. Cathy, they nearly arrested me!'

'Well, my pet, you did start this thing.'

'It wasn't my fault … it just happened. Oh, my sign! I've lost my sign. I must have dropped it over there … where the policeman attacked me. Oh please, Cathy, please fetch it for me.' Now Felicity was crying and wiping the tears from her face. 'But I made it. It's mine. It has my name on the back, and a little one on the front, and also down the handle. It will be easy to find. Please find it, Cathy.'

And so Miss Catherine Dewhirst began the fateful walk onto the erstwhile battlefield which was to determine the events that would fill the remains of their year together.

Catherine walked amongst the detritus of the maelstrom, where all action had ceased, the conflict being brief and one-sided. Where victors milled about uncertainly amongst the broken and discarded accoutrements of the vanquished, the vanquished—who, just a few moments before, had been a diverse but single body of purpose—were now thrown to the winds, the wounded carted to hospital, the captured sent to victor's justice, and the many of the routed now scattered and heading for sanctuary in sympathetic public halls, tea shops or private houses, to complain, to debate, to write letters of protest to the newspapers.

Catherine found the placard, not five paces from some policemen. She picked it up and asked if she might take it. No one answered, so she walked away, stopping momentarily to ask a policeman to what station the arrested would be taken.

A young man rushed up to ask her name and occupation, and being so self-conscious of the situation poor Miss Catherine Dewhirst answered and it was done! A reader might blame Felicity's hand that threw the potato, but their doom was fated by four little words— *Miss Catherine Dewhirst, student.*

Felicity was beside herself. She kissed her friend profusely, said what a hero she was, while holding her placard as a mother holds her baby. They agreed they should attend the police station to assist the woman who had sacrificed herself for Felicity's freedom.

Along the way Felicity stopped and called across the street to a house under construction, to the workmen, and laid down a banter of suffragette slogans and speculations about women commanding the reins of government and society, and a new world where men stayed home and brushed their hair.

There were ironic cheers and a foreman told her to go away. Some crude remarks passed, which Felicity took offense at, protesting that was no way to speak to a woman, a sister, or a prospective wife and mother. A few voices took her part, while other voices became raised in a flow of English and Irish accents, complaining about wages and favouritism. The foreman called for work and calm, and made a threating move toward Felicity, causing her to run up the street, but Catherine stayed, to watch—she saw men coming from all parts of the job, pushing and shaping up, while others cheered for pugilistic action.

Giving up on this nonsense Catherine followed Felicity, and as Catherine approached her friend the last of the daylight caught the street's windowpanes, dissolving them into a pearly effervescence and Felicity into formless darkness.

'What's the matter, Cat?' and Catherine replied, 'Nothing, my pet. Come along. We must try and help your saviour.'

They walked on, Felicity's arm around Catherine's waist, her hand seeking comfort in the movement of Catherine's body as she confessed, 'I kissed Algy by the chicken coop', and Catherine replied, 'Father thought he'd been drinking, but mother said it was just the proximity of a pretty girl. She was right as usual.'

'You are so fortunate to have a mother.'

◆ ◆ ◆

The police station was a squat red brick building with a bell light fixture dangling over the door and footpath. The friends stood on the opposite side of the street, contemplating this institution they had never considered before. A rumbling cavalcade of horse-drawn wagons, motor trucks, omnibuses, cars, and hand-drawn carts passed before them.

'How can it stand it?' Catherine observed. 'Look, Kit, for every two people who go in, only one comes out … Surely the place is going to burst sooner or later.'

'Cathy, you go in. They might recognise me.'

'But you haven't done anything, remember? Besides, you have to assist the woman who helped you. It's your women's creed.'

Catherine tugged Felicity across the street, releasing her so she might place her placard against the station wall so the sign faced inward. They entered into a crowd heavily representative of the toiling classes. Policemen were either hard at work administering the law or loitered with a malevolent boredom. Our heroines passed from one official to another until a clerk recognised the word *suffragette* and said the person they sought was Mrs Edith Sawyer, who had been released. Mrs Sawyer's address was battered out of him by Catherine's eyelashes.

Turning to go, Felicity gasped in horror, for barring their way was the whiskered officer with the steely eyes, minus his hat, the target of Felicity's potato.

Catherine stood looking into the hostile obstacle, while Felicity cringed behind her friend.

'Well, well, look what we have 'ere. The stone thrower of W'ite'all.'

'We were just leaving officer,' Catherine responded, 'and we don't know anything about a stone.'

'Oh, yer don't, do's yer? But I couldn't let you leave, Missy—not after what your little friend done.'

'My friend, Sir, is a silly little virgin. She couldn't do anything. It was you, you and your whistle. They should take it away from you. You are a menace.'

The officer gasped. 'I was on duty, keepin' the peace, protectin' ah civil rights. While your rabble—'

'My rabble, Sir, was trying to win rights for'— Catherine read the police number on his collar—'for your Mrs 14-07. I can only imagine a life of drudgery, looking after you, having your children, what an honour! You should have just one baby, Sir, then tell me how you do not want women to have the same rights as men.'

'That tis poly-tics, Miss. I am above partisanship, but I do pur-sue felons …'

'I will believe that when I see you in the House of Lords, breaking a few skulls during a rowdy debate. Now please, let those who are innocent pass. Then you can get back to protecting the crown jewels, or something even more important!'

'I am on duty, Miss, and I can say, with con-fid-dence, our crown jewels is safe'n sound. But I ain't here to bandy clever words with the likes as you.'

'Then let us pass. As I recall, your latest triumph was over a large lady with an umbrella. And where's your hat, Sir?'

Again the policeman gasped. 'Me hat, Miss, was lost in your little friend's riot.'

'And we say, *your* riot, Sir. And we have no interest in your hat. We shall pass. Then you can resume your duties, chasing villains … protecting property … and, *and persecuting innocent suffragettes.*'

A superior officer hove to and addressed 14-07 about some irrelevant nonsense so that 14-07 was forced to salute and appear to be interested in whatever the nonsense amounted to, which allowed our heroines to slip away, gain the street, whence they proceeded speedily on their way, though halfway across the street Felicity remembered her placard and sped back to retrieve it.

Retrieving her sign, Felicity was confronted again by 14-07. She let out a gasp and ran to the crossing. A motor truck's breaks screeched, and the driver of a wagon reined in his horse so violently sparks flew from beneath its hooves. Miraculously, both machine and horse just avoided bowling over a terrified Felicity.

14-07 let out a cry, but recovering himself, he boomed, 'Stop there, Missy!' and, walking into the street, authoritatively commanded the traffic to halt, and beckoned to Felicity she should proceed in safety.

As she passed, 14-07 remarked, 'Girlie, you can't even cross a street properly.' When Felicity was safely past him, she called back, 'And you can't even arrest a girl.'

The friends parted at Piccadilly Circus, Catherine to her college dormitory and Felicity to her boarding house. While Catherine had an assignment to rush the production of, Felicity entered her room, placed her placard near her bed and lay down to admire it.

Chapter 7.
Fake news

This chapter records how our characters responded to the report of the suffragette/police riot in the Monday morning newspapers.

We start with Reverend Harold Dewhirst.

He was up at six o'clock (three hours before the delivery of the morning newspaper) and bicycled to his church, where he sat on a pew to read the homily he would deliver the following Sunday. It was a peach, corrections unnecessary, conformity to doctrine, perfect— trust in authority: exhibit Jesus's duty to face the cross in obedience to his father's will.

Placing the sermon in the presbytery he cycled back through the town, the wind flowing through his hair and clothes, the swift partnership of bicycle and man animating a quite different Reverend this story is familiar with. Curiously, he was being hailed by parishioners as he swiftly passed them on his way home. As he didn't want to tarry—breakfast was beckoning—he waved back in the spirit he took these odd salutations to be communicated in. He thought the townsfolk's high-spirits must be something to do with the homily he had just composed. Perhaps he was shining with the light of righteousness … though, when you came down to it that was a bit of a long shot. So it just must be one of those days!

Now in the countryside and the delightful passage through woodlands, where a motley of light and shadow flickered and teased him as he cycled through, then out amongst dozing green pastures which he slipped past in a peddling daydream of how he was to spend the next two blissful days devoid of pastoral commitments, barring some village catastrophe such as an illness coming to its ultimatum, or a local girl finding she was pregnant, or one of the leaders of the other denominations wanting a powwow about something ecumenical.

The Reverend Dewhirst was experiencing what is called a heightened reality. Unfortunately the barbarians were already at the threshold of his breakfast table.

Catherine had gone to her rest late, having written all her lecturer had said on a certain topic. Catherine's memory was a prodigious thing, which meant most scholarship was all too easy for Miss Catherine Dewhirst. Of course, there is nothing like having *friends*—friends helped each other, friends eased the way—but Catherine was her own majority and hardly knew a network existed, and so made no use of friends. In the morning she decided to skip the days lectures, deciding instead on a stroll in Hyde Park—what could be more pleasant? She would return to her digs for morning tea in the common room—scones, strawberry jam and cream. Just thinking about it made her say 'Yummy.'

Meanwhile, Felicity got out of bed, looked at her sign, looking at it this way and that before reluctantly dragging herself away. Promenading through a busying London she passed many newsstands, and the call of the newsies, 'READ ALL ABOUT IT! WOMEN'S RIOT IN WHITEHALL. SUFFRAGETTE ATTEMPT TO BURN PARLIAMENT!' made no impression upon her.

Reverend Harold Dewhirst sat down to breakfast at 10.00 a.m., unaware of the discussion in the kitchen between Mrs Dewhirst, cook, and Annie, the morning and evening help—Annie's employment in the Dewhirst household was to be recognised as an act of Christian charity. Cook was to engineer her attendance with a kettle of hot water. Mrs Dewhirst taking her place at table would be the signal for Annie to deliver the newspaper, allowing all interested parties to see the *result of the shot*.

Catherine was drawn into her college's common-room by the enchanting aroma of freshly baked scones. Her fellow students seemed waiting some kind of spectacle. Catherine helped herself to tea, and as she approached the scones, where the daily newspapers were prominently displayed, the students held their breath.

But Catherine confounded the hopes of her audience. Gathering tea, scones, and dollops of toppings, she moved to her usual chair by the window. A girl who was known to be smitten with Catherine was pushed forward and shyly offered her hero the newspaper.

Catherine thanked her.

Felicity was going about her work when her manager slapped the newspaper down in front of her and said, stabbing the front page photograph with her finger, 'Isn't this your beau?'

In the Dewhirst breakfast room, with all interested parties in position, Annie marched in to deliver the morning newspaper.

'What's he doing? There, outside the window?'

'It's the gardener, dear.'

'But it's Monday morning! What's the matter with that man? When you expect him, he's not to be found. Then he appears first thing Monday morning. Staring through the window at me as I take breakfast! He spends most of his time in the tavern, gossiping about us. You don't think he can hear us, do you?'

'He contracted malaria in India.'

'I'm not replying to that, Agnes. I won't fall into one of your Wonderlands. Good God! Look at this. There's been an attempt by suffragettes to burn down the Houses of Parliament. Didn't that Felicity say something about the suffragettes?'

A grave silence followed, before the Reverend Harold Dewhirst almost launched himself into godless space when he read, then re-read, the photographs caption, 'Miss Catherine Dewhirst, student and suffragette.' And there was a photograph, an incontestable photograph plastered across the entire nation, like a bill poster on every street corner of the land. Wearing that stupid hat, looking like an incendiary. The Reverend's mind raced. 'What the——? What!' But it was no good, because there was the incontestable proof, for all the world to see. He was thinking, perhaps I can blame the Jews … but I don't know any Jews. Then perhaps the Masons——no, that might cruel my chances with them … Then what about the Huns? Yes, those brutes are always up to no good. But how did they get at Catherine? They would need a surrogate …

'FELICITY! I knew it! That girl was always out to get us. She is a socialist. An enemy of our ruling class, of Christianity. And wasn't Algy dopey about her? She's stealing our manhood. That makes sense, doesn't it? Oh my. The bishop! The bishop must've seen this … everyone must know …' And the Reverend Dewhirst collapsed back into his chair and stared as if all the world paraded through his imagination as one jury delivering a unanimous verdict of guilty, guilty, guilty.

'Harold, really, this must be a mistake. She was here at Easter, as normal as normal can be. And look, the story and the picture are not really related, are they? Though I must say, it's a splendid photograph of our girl.'

The Reverend looked hopefully at the newspaper as Mrs Dewhirst appealed to Annie. 'You've known our Catherine from childhood. Do you think she would be party to a plot to burn the Houses of Parliament?'

'Oh yes, Madam. She could do anything she'd put her mind to.'

Out of the Reverend's miasma came, 'I've told you before, never to ask Annie's opinion. If you ask her what cheese the moon is made from …'

'I would say—'

'Shut up, Annie. I see your point, about the picture, and the story, but it's too sophisticated. We would have to take each person aside and convince them. But it does give hope. Now … Catherine and normal … normal and Catherine. I think I'm in the Annie camp there. Where's Algy?'

'He left early … to walk Messalina to school.'

'What's the matter with that boy? Always the girls! Agnes, I want you to pack a small suitcase for Algy and me. We are going to sort this out. Hopefully we'll be back later tonight with an explanation we can have a good old fashion laugh about … Now, what is the fastest way to get us to the station?'

The answer came from an unexpected dimension, from the gardener as he leant through the open window and chortled, 'Do't thee worry, mahstur. Oi can take thee in me cahrt.'

As for Catherine, she had dissolved into laughter. Her laughter rolled through all the ramifications, laughing at each one in turn, from, 'My dear Felicity, how do you do it?' through, 'Oh, poor father!' to end with, 'What a bonfire that would be' before biting into a scone and turning the page.

Her audience was offended, perplexed—they hardly thought laughter appropriate—while the smitten girl fainted with frustrated joy as her friends hopped and chirruped about her in a birdlike panic.

It was six o'clock in the evening when the motor taxi dropped Reverend Dewhirst and Algy at Catherine's dormitory, a neoclassical building imposed upon by two monumental Corinthian columns which the Reverend saw as an ill omen, being familiar with *that* ancient temple's *reputation*, and which caused him to shrink with the fear he was not really up to confronting his daughter.

At this very moment Felicity rounded the corner and observed the Dewhirsts' arrival. Choosing a cautious diplomacy, she entered via the service entrance, which took her to the rear of the building and thence into the kitchen, where she commandeered a staff member who escorted her to where the Dewhirsts were having their conference.

Felicity listened at the door whilst holding staff's hand. Staff complained but Felicity insisted, 'You want to earn two shillings, don't you? Then quiet!' and as she listened she heard Catherine explain, 'But father, it's just newspaper talk. This is what they teach me in college.'

'No one teaches this photograph except in the most seditious anarchist cabals. Look, your mother's daughter, flicking her nose at King and country … and our police force! I can only think Felicity is a bad influence.'

'I can honestly say no one has more awe for our police force than Miss Felicity. Father, any accusation against that innocent is unworthy. I can only imagine how she has greeted this news. She is probably thinking of cutting me off, so great is her love of law and order.'

'Well, what on earth were you doing? Look! Your confederates have fled, but you are … there … thumbing your nose …'

'Exactly, father, but not thumbing. I am demonstrating, after the riot. I am alone, making no effort to burn parliament. "Votes for Women" doesn't seem very extreme.'

'But that's not how it looks! It looks … like you've gone mad … and are challenging the entire … social order! And that hat—that hat makes you look … suggests, you are a new Britannia!'

'Then I'm unjustly accused. I cannot confess, so I must offer penance. I will gladly resign my position in the women's movement if it would appease my dear father. I will gladly spurn the journalists who have sought my intellectual perspective …'

'Journalists? Journalists! You cannot compound this misfortune with more newspaper talk … can you? Will you? No, I've thought about this—'

'Perhaps I should come home and face the music.'

'You are mad! No, you need to get away. You need a rest. Bruges …'

'Not Bruges!'

'Then Paris, with Cousin Gerald, to continue your education.'

'Cousin Gerald! I hardly think that would be the right education.'

'Now, don't be like that. Gerald is roundly misunderstood. You would do well to discount gossip and judge for yourself. Algy, where's the envelope? Here's twenty-five …'

A door opened and staff was pushed in. 'Miss Catherine, I'm having some trouble with the kettle, or something. Would you spare a minute to help me?'

Catherine, leaving the envelop, exited, whence Felicity, in one movement, pressed two shillings into staff's hand and grabbed Catherine. 'You must ask for fifty pounds,' whispered Felicity.

'You! Do you see what's happened to me?'

'It's done, so why worry? But I have fifty pounds. If you can get that much, we can go to Italy. Don't you want to have a spring, a long lazy summer and autumn in Italy with your Kit, and with the greatest art of the Renaissance and the ancient world?'

'How did you get fifty pounds …?'

'Some savings too, but I couldn't refuse. The painter was one of the most expensive in London. I sent Lord Somersby a watercolour sketch of myself. Not in the best taste. I was a simpleton servant, on a ladder dusting a chandelier, and it was a hot day. It cost a guinea, as a thank-you for our visit. And he requested I sit for a portrait … but now you need to get passage to Italy. If you want to, my dear, true love …'

Catherine returns: 'I am sorry for the adjournment. What were we discussing … journalists?'

'NO! We were agreeing you need to get away. We agree there is nothing substantial in this scandal, but we agreed your absence from the stage is a fitting remedy.'

'I can see the wisdom in your thinking, father. On my return you will kill the fatted calf, for I know I will be all the better for my short exile.'

Reverend Dewhirst didn't like his daughter using scripture, nor was he game to point out her use of it was not entirely *germane* to the situation. As usual he was torn between believing she cared and fearful of what she had in reserve, which is why he didn't correct her parabolic fancy. He was now in the familiar position of seemingly having an advantage, which only too predictably would be snatched away.

Catherine: 'If I'm going to follow your advice and start a less formal education, offstage, then I will endeavour to make you proud of your prodigal daughter.'

Again, her dubious scripture! He felt the urge to raise his voice and declare her use of the parable a corruption. He wanted his daughter to be guilty, and contrite, and not escape into a future … *celebration* … But the Reverend's knees were beginning to sag with the encounter, with the effort to suppress his rage, and he was hoping the bell was going to beat the sucker punch he felt was ready to be let loose. Again he turned to Algy, but before he could request the envelope …

'To be safe, I think I'll need only a further twenty five pounds, if I stay for six months. And I should take French lessons. If so, I will mail you.'

'Sister, do you think we have time to call on Felicity? We are planning to take the eight o'clock from Euston Station.'

'My dear, precious Algy. Oh course, Felicity would be delighted to see you. If you are walking from here it's on your way. You will have bags of time. She would be devastated if you don't call in … she did enjoy the Dewhirst family so. You will find her at a club called The Grosvenor, Piccadilly Square. Through the tavern, and the club is upstairs. You will find her there in all her glory.'

The Reverend had given up. He wrote a note to his bank, and took solace in at least getting what he thought was the best possible result. Yet he wondered whether something was behind all this—perhaps Catherine was the Kaiser's agent after all, and was now going to do something dastardly to the French.

'Do you think Algy will want me as his fiancé when he sees my picture?' Felicity asked as the friends walked arm in arm to a restaurant, to plan their great Italian adventure.

'I can assure you he most definitely will, though I wonder what father will think.'

Father and son climbed the stairs and explained to the concierge they were only there to see Miss Felicity. Curiously, the concierge was most encouraging, though slightly enigmatic with his salutation of, 'Never too young to put the boy right, eh, gov'nah?'

Reverend Dewhirst and Algy stood looking up at a nude Felicity, erstwhile lover of law and order, their speechlessness appropriate to the subject of their gaze.

It was Algy who broke the silence, but not the spell, with, 'It's what Felicity said at lunch. Remember when she demonstrated modelling … she had the same kind of commitment then, as is there. It is a talent.'

'Yes, yes. I see you are right. She conveys to me … how sad is this beautiful girl loitering in a harem, denied a freedom which should be her right. Perhaps your sister is right … protesting for the rights of women and a better, if not perfect world. Now Algy, we must go. We have a train to catch.'

Chapter 8.
Edith

The friends planned a feint to Paris, an interview with Cousin Gerald, before explaining Catherine's leaving for Italy as an opportunity too good to miss— the opportunity to be embroidered with an educative theme.

Before crossing to France they needed to enquire after the suffragette who had sacrificed herself for Felicity's freedom.

On a drizzling English morning our heroines stood before the scarlet door of No. 46, Waterloo Square— a grand terrace house with a classically ornamented porch composed of columnettes, pilasters, and entablatures with friezes and cornices et al., which was just one of many similar houses, lining the four sides of Waterloo Square.

Doughnutted by this quadrangle of residences lay a private park, high-fenced and locked, a paradise only the residents of Waterloo Square, or their guests, had a right and key to enter, where, I imagine, these blessed could promenade at their leisure, safe to push their prams or greet their blessed neighbours, perhaps to read the stock market news or sit in contemplation under dappled shade, snug in the belief they were ruled by common sense, while their children bowled their hoops or threw their balls, anxiously lest complaint was raised due to their boisterousness.

Behind No. 46's scarlet door lived Felicity's saviour, Mrs Edith Sawyer, dowager, fermented anarchist, amoralist, who would blow everything of our heroines' adventure and friendship sky-high. The crazy endeavours of the widow Sawyer would bestow upon our heroines mild and temporary infamy.

'My word, yes, I do recognise you, my dear, dear comrade, from the front pages of the daily newspaper,' Mrs Sawyer said in greeting, embracing Catherine as if a long-lost daughter, while addressing Felicity somewhat as if examining an unfamiliar species and waiting upon the determination of what the thing was.

Edith pressed on with her effusive endearments, which were both intimate and distant.

'Life's a journey,' Edith declared, without thought as to the stillborn, nor the world's slaves, nor the starving poor, nor the bullies, the creeps and the violent unremorseful criminal need bother themselves to comprehend just what a 'life's journey' actually might be—though it seemed to promise, for a certain kind, a purpose and an arrival hinting at a homecoming.

Edith ploughed on in monologue, revealing as much penetration of her subjects as a viewer is offered by the esteemed figures in a waxworks, our heroines' critical faculties so overwhelmed by quantity they could only listen in respectful silence.

Having worn herself out Mrs Sawyer bid her guests sit themselves in the parlour as her butler was ordered to bring tea.

The parlour was not the height of fashion, but a once rich old bird plucked of its feathers—guilty shadows on the walls, places where potted greenery attempted to hide a missing something. The antics of a parrot standing on its cage and censoriously referred to by the Mistress as *Teutonic*, momentarily entertained.

'Cads! Bounders! The lot of them. I'm talking about the House of Lords … the Commons! A matter for the firing squad. I say … it is you, isn't it? From that jingoistic, imperialist rag, whatsisname. The suffragette, who tried to burn the Houses of Parliament. Bravo! Let's celebrate … a little snifter anybody? Got me own El Dorado here … ha ha … secret from old *horse face*'—indicating the door whence exited the butler.

And their hostess lifted a bottle from the umbrella stand and leered, 'Top-notch brandy, anyone? … Well, I don't mind as I do. A cure for all ailments … wonderful stuff. Not for your pew-fillers, stuffed shirts, if you know what I mean.'

'Oh, yes, that!'—apropos of rescuing Felicity from the constabulary—'Just an excuse to clobber one of the blighters. I've been arrested sooooo many times. In gaol … so wonderful to get out. Like, like crawling out of a grave, I can tell you … the worst of it … those suffering suffragettes … tiresome! Sooooo, sooo earnest, beee-yond tolerance. The influence of the Teetotallers, and the church, I'm sure. They say the poor will always be with us, but I could do without the bluestockings. Give me the poor any day … at least they can hold a grudge. Still, it's not a real world where one can choose one's allies.'

'Journalism, do you say … well, it's so difficult to get ideas in print. New ideas, I mean; ideas that really matter. And you there, selling hats. Well done! That's important too. One can always tell … who one is talking to by the shine of their shoes or the cut of their hat. It's the small things, you know. Did you say you were off to the Continent … My, what a slave market that must be.'

A thoughtful pause, before … 'A tour of the Continent! My lord, what a campaign you are engaged upon. Real Livingston stuff! The Continent's women are rotting in their clothes. Slaves to male chauvinism and privilege. They don't even let them wash, so as I hear. I say … we must continue the crusade. Yes … I have a cousin at the Daily Mail. We might … swing, an article, a series of articles … based on your tour … a commentary on women's issues on the continents. Magnificent! Yes, now I think on it, you might even be paid for your work, if it's newsworthy, if you know what I mean. Sensational! Hard-hitting.'

Without labouring this narrative further, a tacit alliance was entered into, born of a mind awash with brandy and insurrection, and agreed to by the other party, who had done their duty and, though fascinated to passivity, were eager to withdraw.

An agent from the *Daily Mail* met our heroines at the railway station and delivered two small parcels. The first, an instruction to capitalise on the notoriety of the suffragettes and to report on the condition of Continental females and gender inequality, reports which might receive *consideration*—the articles should have a negative slant in comparison to the English sisterhood. He seemed to think Catherine was a working journalist.

Catherine suggested as a nom de guerre *Pandora,* to which the agent sneezed—or was it a giggle, Catherine records. In the fullness of time she would find it was the latter.

The second was a sealed envelope, within an appeal by Mrs Sawyer to forward the articles to her for editing, dots and dashes et al., thence she would submit it to the newspaper, by hand, via her cousin, thus giving a greater chance of success.

'Family matters, my dear,' she wrote, 'and my family have been depriving the talented and righteous of places where sense should have prevailed for hundreds of years. You'll find genius matters in history books but, day to day, in the here and now, it's working the system that counts. I could tell you some pathetic stories … but it doesn't seem to have done much harm. Be stoic, runs on the board, that's what I say. It's nature! Let me take care of the *access* side of things. You just produce some entertainments, and we'll have their heads off in no time.'

In Paris Catherine wrote her first article, including a bibliography of persons she'd spoken to and women's organisation she'd consulted.

Catherine eventually discovered Cousin Gerald, who escorted them to places where household domestics and other drudges sought their entertainments. Catherine gave stark testimony to issues of female domestic's vulnerability to the sexual advances of their employers, and issues of paternity.

Felicity spent her days in the galleries, eventually finding a costume in an old wares shop and accompanying Catherine and Gerald.

What did they look like in those boisterous taverns of the Parisienne working poor—the fluent dapper English gent, the earnest enquiring English girl and, hanging off her arm, an artist's idealised 18th-century milkmaid with blond plaits, dressed in red and white gingham?

Chapter 9.
Springtime in Italy with the Contessa Polissema de Vasari

The bulging girth of Hotel Superba spread itself about Via Garibaldi, gorging on tourists like a glutton at a banquet's hors d'oeuvres … and disgorging them into the street like the sophisticated establishment it was. Florentine pedestrians venturing near surrendered their rights of safe passage to its bulk, making their way via a sliver of footpath and the precarious edge of the road.

Built in the cinquecento to shelter a great family whose patriarchs beavered away acquiring wealth, power and esteem, while in their leisure they indulged themselves and worried about their soul. The family expressed piety by giving alms to the poor and donations to a wealthy church, complaining about licentious monks and nuns run amuck, about whores in the Vatican, and when will Michelangelo finish his work in the Vatican chapel for the glory of their Saviour, the world-loving God? The Superba was built as a stronghold against the murderous plots of their worldly neighbours, who also worshipped the same world-loving God. In their day, palaces like the Superba declared safety from the internecine hatred flowing and ebbing about the streets.

But the Hotel Superba was not the place of rest for our heroines—they rested at a more humble establishment near train station Maria Antonia—but after a day's wandering they would retire to the Superba to enjoy afternoon tea and luxuriate in the first-class conveniences.

Whilst taking tea at the Superba they met Henry and Audrey, a honeymooning English couple.

Audrey's father had arranged for the couple to be chaperoned by a local Anglophile, the Contessa Polissema de Vasari, who, while extending her salutations to the couple, had observed Catherine and suggested the invitation to her Villa Vasari might also include these English girls.

The Contessa was to prove invaluable in the composition of Catherine's articles, as well as being the subject of the last, which would prove a coup de grâce to their adventure.

(I remind you of my assertion, in the Apologia, that Catherine's descriptions are idiosyncratic, as our detour to the Superba illustrates. The Contessa, though long passed, was to provide me with the most exquisite artefact of my heroines' time together, its provenance and attribution of subject lost to history, but restored by me in composing this story—this related far below ☺)

The Villa Vasari was located in the rural wilds surrounding Florence, our party carried there in the Contessa's aged barouche and pair.

Catherine worried aloud their barouche was bearing a privileged four pasta toiling world of rustic poverty. That whatever qualities they possessed was eclipsed by their voyeurism. Henry said Catherine was mistaken; saying their gawking probably wasn't the worst thing about them. Catherine agreed, and suggested a competition whereby they might expiate this frivolous blot by confessing a sin that was worthy of confession and judgment.

Catherine presented first, admitting to deceiving fifty pounds from her father, a man of the cloth, for an education in France, only to elope with Felicity to Italy. The newlyweds gasped at this dishonour.

Felicity confessed to being truly common, for she had barged her way into life via illicit ways and endured all the frights of powerlessness until arriving at the lucrative enterprise of selling views of her trinkets for a pittance to any well-paying copyist. Henry sought clarification, to which Felicity replied her copyists would hardly be interested in her clothes.

Audrey professed to being innocent, that having a benevolent father must be a reward, so she must endure the brand of gawker, and although she empathised with Felicity, must contradict her, having recently discovered how pleasant is her powerlessness and her newly discovered trinkets.

Henry confided his anxieties about marrying into wealth, which the object of his desire had delivered— he wished she were a milkmaid like the girls in the landscape, rather than an heiress. Yet he had the woman he loved, and his punishment would be the albatross from his father-in-law, the pipes that would be his main subject of study and conversation from now till the day he died. He shuddered to think of the minds he would have to converse with, about pipes and the things they would transport…water, gas, and unmentionables. It was cruel fate, being all decided, like an animal in Africa, knowing your destiny was to be killed and eaten; that all your days were to be spent musing like an idiot, about these pipes until the inevitable, fatal ambush.

'What kind of man betrays his self?' Henry declared.

Audrey cleaved to her husband—and would have clung if Henry was not opposite her in the barouche and secured with Felicity's arm entwining his—saying true love made her husband sacrifice his intellectual freedom to make her happy—and Felicity would do as she had to, to sup with one wolf to keep the others from the door, but Catherine was the only one truly saved from being a voyeur, as she was truly wicked.

Felicity insisted Catherine was redeemed by her efforts to reformation of the world, by holding a candle to reveal the slavery of women.

Catherine: 'It's true. But am I not exploiting the misery of the world by my journalism? Hiding my wickedness behind a display of concern for the exploited?'

Audrey: 'Of course you are … but I hear the guilty should always fain innocence.'

The barouche swung into the driveway of the Villa Vasari, farewelling the open road like an inebriated fat man tarrying on the verge to raise his hat to a contemptuous neighbour, before heaving its slatternly guts onto the driveway, puffing with wobbly care through a crumbling stone gateway surmounted by a lightning-blasted tableaux of the Holy Trinity, and then, as the authority of gravity lessened with a flatter surface, skipped with renewed vigour along the carriage ruts, over the lush ribbon of driveway grass, betwixt an avenue of raggedy poplar trees, its mission to convince as a guard of honour—though now, one in a distant and half-forgotten outpost of empire where the light of the central authority shone not brightly. Still, this avenue of neglect was effective in articulating the grand finale, the Villa Vasari, by casting a spell of delight upon each traveller as they imagined themselves as important persons, who were soon to be in the presence of greatness.

Who would have suspected our pair, too, would be deeply moved by their expectation of viewing the villa's 17th-century façade, for with each stride the horses transferred a burst of enthusiasm to the barouche so the driver swore as he tried to rein in his charges.

As our barouche clattered passed the villa, the old dear woke from its slumber, looked down its serpentine steps and frowned, 'Who needs you, you who do not even suspect my divine proportions?'

The friends must have felt the condescension; their heads turned regretfully as they realised they were never to enter via those fine steps.

'Surely,' a passenger worried as they flew past, 'our host can't live in a hovel out back … do you think?'

For the old dear's front doors had been closed for centuries and would only be reopened by the work of students of architecture who, even as our heroines careered by, were writing articles and chapters to make Villa Vasari famous once more—that is, a fine example of its type of historic building, built so the fine people of the day might promenade in a refined rural setting discussing opera, art, and philosophy—but behind which now was carried out the keeping and slaughter of cows and goats, and strangling of chickens for *cacciatora*.

The carriage rattled though a new entrance, a mere century old barchessa, a paved courtyard surrounded by high walls pierced with spaces for agrarian activity. As our party decamped, a menial beckoned them to follow through a high stone barrel vault where many birds loudly celebrated their home, and after exiting this symphony were greeted by an Arcadian landscape rolling into the distant haze, while the Villa Vasari sat lordly on its stone dais, commanding this vista.

Our travellers climbed the lichen-stained steps to the terrace where the Contessa waited, leaning her back against the balustrade, as tranquil as a garden statue, and wrapped in black lace like a little raincloud edged by pristine morning sunlight that gathered to her by her occasional jewellery and sparkling eyes. Her head leant to one side, enquiringly, her arms folded upon her waist, both characteristics of her when still. Her coloured lips, like the Syren call on a gloomy night, captured straight the visitors, and drew them to her.

The Contessa offered her hand to each, declared how happy she was to welcome her guests, that she had forever wished she were a sensible English lady and henceforth would speak only English, and she would be pleased if they corrected her as she paddled about their language, no matter how slight was her blunder. When the Contessa smiled her eyes became crescent moons.

Morning tea for five was ordered by the hostess, her crescent moons delighting in the incongruity of this English ritual she advised would go bung on her villa's terrace.

'All this,' the hostess declared, 'and we only make a livelihood for our tenants! No wonder the English laugh at us.'

The hostess prepared her guests to expect anything in the way of cake, explaining it was an expression of cook's patriotism—'Some things I am powerless. I would try beating her, but it would only make dust'—as her eyes passed into the distance behind Catherine.

Cook turned out to be the Contessa's mother.

The hostess attended to each newlywed with teasing metaphor of thinly veiled carnality, imploring them to love and be loved, and to forgive. An attempt reciting Shakespeare's Henry VI, a planned failure, she beseeched Henry to finish (To be no better than a homely swain …), so pleasing to the hostess she produced an anthology of the great poet, each taking a turn reading to a Contessa enraptured to silence.

I paraphrase Catherine by remarking the Contessa was dark, her skin an olive tan, a sad hunger inhabiting her slender but vibrant frame … although as a whole one was struck by a great collection of parts, as if the creator, after toiling all day, was left with a box of spares—a tiny waist, narrow feminine shoulders and boyish hips—and threw them together declaring, 'That's a girl.' In movement, languid and spare; at rest, merging with the contours she rested upon. No one sat on a chair like the Contessa Vasari … except, perhaps, an octopus.

And if anyone could effortlessly ride a giant clam shell to shore it was their hostess, though as Donatello's David and not the voluptuous original.

The Contessa was lowborn to a hovel. After a series of adventures fending off the advances of lusty men— including one she brained with a skillet so he was never the same again—she was controversially elevated by marriage to the Count. The family found they liked her, and had use for her charisma and in keeping the Count away from the family fortunes.

An enquiry about the absence of the Count was explained as a faux pas, that might force an Italian wife to lie, but she would boldly address the truth, which the Contessa understood to be the English style. The Contessa declared her husband, who was considerably older than she, had found his Aphrodite in an alpine barn. The maid had the body of a Venus de Milo with the arms of a wrestler. He is happy, she said, which she implored to be a lesson to us all … just as long as they stayed in the mountains. This hung in the air as if happiness, if one sought this idyll, was forever under threat from tomorrow.

Lunch was laid beneath a vine-laden trellis, the travellers being joined by three young gentlemen, and a monk.

The lunch was gay, with the Italian speakers being inquiring and ingratiating, although not possessing the Contessa's amusing philosophy. When the Contessa was momentarily called away Catherine noted a subtle altering of tone in a few Italian sentences, and though she saw it, she did not register alarm at a hand tarrying briefly over a glass of wine.

The Contessa excused herself from the after-lunch walk to an ancient Roman ruin a mile distant. On their return she would take afternoon tea with her guests … she would bake scones for them, an act they were to understand by her grave change in demeanour as heroic with a real chance of failure, and then see them on their way … saying perhaps they might reacquaint soon in Firenze.

After the party set off Felicity grew pensive and wan, complained she needed to rest, perhaps the heat was the cause—and her face did appeared flushed. A flourish of voices decided Felicity should return to the villa, safely escorted by the concerned monk. The rest would strike out for the ruin, which was a most atmospheric marvel, and easily within reach for a quick return home. And so the party split into two, but with each step Catherine grew less interested in the ruin and more concerned by her friend's distemper, until she confided her fears to Audrey, who advised if she felt so unnerved, then what is seeing a ruin to that? With this advice Catherine fell back; pretending to examine some wildflowers she slipped away, hastening back to the villa, there asking a servant where the English lady had been taken. The servant preceded Catherine up a staircase to a second-floor room, which he indicated but did not enter, wherein Catherine discovered Felicity sleeping peacefully on a divan. Catherine's anxiety was resolved, and she waited upon her friend's revival, examining the antique room, the faded painted narratives on the walls, the cracked plaster of the ceiling. The few pieces of furniture did not encroach on the pleasing emptiness. The chairs could be moved around to take advantage of the windows, the fire, or the desk standing by itself before a bookcase. At last, Catherine thought, taking note of the casual neglect and the unfamiliar lines and fillings of the room, I am in a foreign country. Selecting an illustrated book she settled into a high-backed chair standing before the cold fireplace. A tall mirror speckled with age hung above the fire surround. Either side of the chimney breast tall windows offered a darkening light and views of the driveway poplars.

Catherine's book caressed her mind, thence to a surrender akin to the phenomenon of sleep, into which we all secretly stumble, no matter if we are angel or daemon, to witness the strangest book we will ever read, stranger still as we have composed the strange narrative ourselves—a museum of absurd junk, anxious confessions, enigmatic truths, and the poetic confusions of ego.

Just as Catherine was to let go a creak prevented the fall, and her sacred sight opened amongst the old mirror's ghostly stigmatisms, to see there a wood panel open at the far side of their room, whence a figure slowly emerged, like a butterfly emerges out of its chrysalis. It grew into a form without wings, wearing a cloak and a mask with a nose curved up and erect.

Catherine watched, disbelieving, as the figure manifested into full form, and moved like mist to linger over the sleeping Felicity.

Without thinking Catherine selected from the fireplace's utensils a sword for her left hand and a poker for her right. She advanced unseen to the visitant that was now hovering over the sleeping Felicity, and stabbed its buttock with the sword.

The figure yelped, turned to see the poker crash into its mask, breaking the nose. With a groan the creature fell backwards and hit the floor, only to revive and turn angrily upon the assailant, but Catherine had again raised the sword so it was pointing at the thing's heart, and the poker was also offering another smiting.

The creature understood the hopelessness of its predicament, and calculating the expression of its hatred might mean the end of all, crawled backwards as Catherine advanced over its retreat. Without rising, the creature disappeared whence it had come, into the wood panels of the wall.

'Kitten, wake up.'

'Maudi, is it you? Come and hide with me, dearie.'

'Kit, we must go now. Can you stand?'

'Oh, Cat … lay down with me. Hold me, my love. I don't want to go.'

'We must go. I will help you stand. Come now, Kit.'

They met the Contessa in the barchessa and seeing Felicity's state she called for a carriage.

'What a day of calamities! And my monk has injured himself falling down the stairs. Why must Italian men carry knives? And a monk too!'

The Contessa noticed Catherine's coldness, her lack of response, and as the carriage arrived she helped load Felicity. As if details which had been disparate now coalesced into one narrative, the appalled hostess assured them she would see their friends returned safely to their hotel, and she took off a bracelet and wrapped it around Felicity's wrist as an act of solidarity and penance, and sadly bid Catherine '*Ciao, bella.*'

'There is nothing to do there, (the Contessa's estate on the Adriatic coast) except pick grapes, swim in the ocean and eat … I will cook for you. But one thing is true, my friends: you cannot go to Rome in high summer. Tourists die there, and even the Romans suffer. And these essays … I will help, Catarina. We can make them up together. With an idiot husband like mine I know many things, including just how stupid women have to be to get anything! You understand, I don't include myself … family. So much property, and the appearance. But I am fortunate. I've avoided my husband, and any talk is, how you say, hushed. Don't worry *fidanzata*'— this to

Felicity—'it's the name and the property they respect.'

As the Contessa is getting into her carriage, Felicity calls from the balcony, 'I am more than … *fidanzata*'. The Contessa: '*Quindi, le signore inglesi fanno risse per strada.*'

And so the three became, like Botticelli's graces, linked empathetically with a staring recognition of each to the other, with holding of hands, through the last of spring and the first of summer, waiting out the Roman plagues, enjoying the Contessa's largess.

Catherine and the Contessa created two articles about the courting and marriage of Italian girls, and the experience post-marriage, but preying on Catherine's mind were two little dramas she had witnessed.

From a train's window I see a small sturdy mother, with a young son in hand, decamp from a train. She busily organises the bags which evidences the journey they have returned from. Her husband, a small man of humble means, approaches, the boy rushes towards him and is gathered akimbo in father's loving arms. He turns about, and father and son set off embracing gleefully, leaving the wife on the platform, forgotten, crushed. Her shoulders sag. Life leaves her as clearly as a breeze passes through a tree. This denial of a welcome is the mother's reality, an anonymous working life of drudgery.

A French tourist family walk past a beggar woman sitting on the footpath with a bawling baby. Only the daughter, in her early teens, ribbons in her hair and wearing a handsome smock, notices and stops before the beggar woman, staring down at her as if uncomprehending of the scene. She cannot move as she tries to understand what she is seeing until a family member calls, 'Alex, come on.' Alexandra skips away to re-join her family … in a thoughtful way.

In Rome the Contessa arranged digs in a relative's palazzo—a massive palace they disappeared into, never meeting their hosts or any of the family, occasionally passing a servant somnambulating along the endless shadow-hung corridors who took no notice of them, or trying to chat to the ever-present doorman, who offered only obsequious bows and smiles. Their room was huge, dark and empty, and furnished with one large bed and an ancient wardrobe. Lamps lit the room by night and by day a barred and shuttered window looking over the street allowed in slashes of sunlight.

As Catherine and Polly worked on an essay about Italian women who chose not to marry, Felicity suggested they should contact the British Embassy—perhaps they might have mail, or read an English newspaper.

From the Embassy they received three letters, each containing a note amounting to twenty-five pounds, and news of the sensation caused by Catherine's articles, that more was desired post haste.

'Twenty-five pounds!' Felicity exclaimed, 'Dearest Cat, what did you put in those stories?'

'I wrote the truth. I am most surprised the truth was so warmly received. In fact, Flick, perhaps I should become a journalist, for it does seem the world is ready for a fine reformation.'

But all was not well … Felicity orders Catherine to comb the Contessa's perfume from her hair before she comes to bed. They argue about leaving for Greece.

Felicity believes she is powerlessness. Another article is started, 'A conversation with an observant Italian lady', being a record of Catherine's conversations with the Contessa, who is, fortuitously, unnamed. This published article seems largely unaltered by Edith: the Contessa putting forward some radical ideas and justifying them as cures for real social ills in a way which highlights the ills rather than the extravagant cures, e.g. castration after siring four children.

The Contessa arranges for the girls to sit for a portrait. Felicity thinks this is a stratagem to keep them in Rome, and so the girls sit, but leave before the painting is finished. No artist's name is recorded in Catherine's journal.

They leave for Napoli, Salerno, and Paestum. Some terrible moments, it seems …

Chapter 10.
Real deportation

This is the background to what happened:

Catherine's articles, published under her own name, created the kind of sensation that sold many newspapers but made no one happy. This unhappiness even travelled to the Italian Minister of Culture, informing him of the damage done to the undisputed *felicita* of Italian womanhood ...

The Carabinieri caught our heroines at Brindisi as they were boarding a steamer to Greece, and ordered their return to Rome, to report to the British Embassy.

In Rome, Catherine endured a lecture by an official of the government in fast-running Italian. The seated

British official suffering a headache as he winced with every crescendo, of which there were four to every minute—the agony compounded by a language he didn't understand.

The English interpreter started proudly, translating every word, but soon fell behind and slipped into speaking keywords, like 'revolutionaries', 'anarchists', and 'witches from hell', but eventually lost his comprehension, giving up when the official started orating to a bare wall where he seemed to see something manifested, whether it was an image of his sainted mother, a haloed Madonna, or a buttery bambino Jesus it was hard to tell, but it did preoccupy him and caused tears to rise in his eyes and rendered his voice with emotion to near breaking. Evidently, Catherine was despicable compared to whatever was there on the wall, and he would wave a newspaper article at her as evidence.

At last the official scrunched up the article, dramatically threw it aside, drew out a kerchief and dabbed his eyes and forehead, signifying he had said all he intended to say on whatever subject he had been addressing.

The British official had suffered greatly and looked to the translator to convey, on behalf of the empire, his heartfelt platitudes, as the representative of the

Italian administration withdrew. Felicity awoke to the resigned tones of the official informing Catherine she had insulted an allied nation, ordering her to take passage, with her companion, on the next British ship to leave for home …

Felicity protested provision should be made for their travel, suggesting passage and ten pounds each should be adequate so British citizens should not be perceived as beggars. Passage and five pounds each was agreed upon and a note was writ—the back and forth negotiations further exasperating the official and covering Catherine's souveniring of the discarded article.

As Catherine passed through the library she searched out her other works and ripped them from their newspapers.

In their hotel Catherine and Felicity read her published articles. It was apparent Felicity's saviour, Edith, had played the main part in making them notorious by her sensationalist interpolations.

Catherine noted the authorities seemed to ignore Edith's lies, but were angered by Polly's truths, from the last article, writing aphoristically, 'The truth seems to be a very powerful poison which is bound to do no one any good. And they say Mr Jesus will come again, but I have my doubts. If he has any sense and does not want the same again, he will stay well away.'

Felicity: 'Oh look! … an invitation to dine with that charming Italian official. Do you see, Cat, there's good in everyone … what matters is the scenario one finds them in!'

On board ship our heroines experienced mild shunning. Invitations were not extended and pleasantries exchanged at a minimum, where avoidance was not practicable. Catherine spent her time thinking and was very quiet, looking out to sea at the interminable waves, which reminded her of endless repetition and meaningless variety.

Felicity talked of their adventure and wondered what was to become of her now. Selling hats and keeping shop seemed a bleak task for one who had travelled the back roads of the Adriatic coast like a gypsy, clambered over the ruins of Rome like a goat, and promenaded through Europe's great museums of art as a posing aesthete.

Reverend Eustace Clayhorn had been informed of the brown-haired girl's notoriety. Amongst the ship's passengers, to which he was a deacon of rectitude, he likely counselled understanding and tolerance, and was determined to make their acquaintance, just the four of them—the dark one, the fair one, his reverence, and the good book.

On a day when the ship was shattering its way through the grey-green sea the Reverend happened upon our heroines as they lounged on deck. Around them a wide arc of empty deckchairs which allowed a strategic intimacy. Reverend Eustace bowed, introduced himself, and seemed to hesitate, as if deciding which of the two was the most attractive.

Soon enough the Reverend was away, enquiring of their sojourn, of which our heroines were only the least bit forthcoming. A careless enquiry had the Reverend declaiming on his exciting travels in Greece, how he had climbed the steps to the Acropolis and counted the stones of the Parthenon's base exactly. How his guide was an ignorant wretch who clambered for money. That he owed it all to his generous benefactor, a titled widow of his parish, who had recognised his enthusiasm for history and ancient culture. In fact, he wrote every day to her of his adventures, and she had replied his correspondence should be published in a stylish magazine. He intended to write a paper explicating the concurrency of pagan and revelatory culture, explaining the former's failure and ruin as an overly secular and sensory focused culture, lacking true morality.

Catherine asked what a culture should be other than a focus on whatever is its secularity. Our Reverend replied, with restrained condescension, the tome she was reading was proof enough; that Ovid's 'Metamorphoses' was so inferior to our 'Paradise Lost' that any comparison was laughable.

Catherine replied, 'No "Metamorphoses", no "Paradise Lost", which is apt.'

The Reverend decided his best chance to impress was with the dumb one.

He now launched his little crusade, confessing he'd dedicated his life to bringing *the good book's* redemptive power to all who most needed its spiritual light. He had seen great transformations amongst sinners willing to turn toward the truth—all it takes is strength of character and an open heart to ask for forgiveness, 'And don't we all need to be forgiven?'

Felicity responded, 'Yes, I have read your book, and how interesting it is, only … I didn't much like the Jesus character.'

'What? What are you saying!' the Reverend, dismayed.

'Felicity means she had trouble with his entourage. Isn't that right, Kit? Anyone would look good next to that cast. To think, he trusted them with the understanding and recording of his life! It's best not to think about it.'

'Do you know, Reverend,' Catherine continued, 'Felicity and I were recently discussing miracles … since we've been travelling we haven't lost a penny of what we started with. What do you say about that!'

Felicity: 'And my Cat is wholly innocent of the charges against her. And if God's on his throne he knows this to be so … no matter what the ignorant believe.'

The Reverend hit out with a strident, 'It is our responsibility to make sure our good name is not allowed to be sullied.'

Catherine: 'And it worked so well for your Jesus. Tell us, Reverend, how did you *really* forsake your flock for Greece? Did you smash open the poor box and stuff the halfpennies into your pocket before fencing the church silver and making away?'

'What-a-suggestion! Outrageous!'

Felicity: 'My dear Puss, you misjudge, for I think I know what's going on. Our aspiring feullitonist is now travelling back to his admirer, to make an honest woman of her. How romantic! You, Sir, have come to your senses, realising you can't live without her, and are prepared to face the consequences.'

'Outrageous! My benefact—my, Mrs … the Duchess, has no such hopes. Mrs … is purely … respect and, and support, in the name of scholarship, only.'

Felicity: 'I bet,' while Catherine painted a picture of the abandoned Mrs, strolling her woe through her allegorical garden. A single crystalline tear falls, and lands hopefully upon her favourite rose, only to slide off a golden downy petal to the sordid earth. Mrs's garden beds, tended with hope and love, manifesting her passion in the profusion of colour and variety, would now fall, like the ancient societies, into ruin from lack of belief and worship … 'But suddenly, Useless bounds into the garden, throws himself at the feet of Mrs and declares, "Can't you see I love you, and I've come to face the consequences?"''

Felicity: 'And the Duchess will be near fainting. With the last of her overpowered sensibilities, Mrs declares, "My one and only Useless! The poor box will be repaired and stuffed to bursting with halfpennies. The church silver will be reclaimed from your tawdry fence, and a new, bigger, better, and older church built to celebrate our love."''

Clayhorn: 'No, you've got it all wrong … scandalously wrong. I never, ever—'

Felicity: 'Then you are in excellent company, not only with your Jesus, but also with my beautiful Cat, who has also been grievously wronged.'

Felicity: 'Isn't it so, Puss, one broadens the mind with travel? And one meets souls that are most harmonious with one. Take Useless—once met, a friend forever.'

Catherine: 'Hey-Ho, we only have to visit his church and, "Hail there, good old Useless, friend forever." He shall be so happy to see us …'

Felicity: 'Hey-Ho, Useless, would you marry us, just your dear friends and the Lord above, what? How could he say no?'

Catherine: 'I'm afraid, my precious kitten, disappointment awaits you. Useless is Eustace, and is powerless to assistus.'

Chapter 11.
Winter, again

Catherine's description of their break is just a few notes. I will take the opportunity to augment these, with some unused material from the journal. I hope the constructed narrative stands in for fact, and conveys a convincing denouement of our protagonist's friendship:

Catherine, entering their London boarding house, is hailed by Charles Broadmoor—a gent we met at the Dewhirst Easter luncheon. Charles has kept up with Catherine's adventures via Algy's correspondence with Felicity. Catherine agreed to walk out, the cold weathering day asserting itself over the fading enchantment of the Mediterranean sun.

Felicity returns early from job seeking. She walks by Catherine's trunk on the footpath and surprises her friend readying for departure.

'I'm going to see Charles's parents. I have left you our monies. Almost one hundred pounds. It is a miracle, isn't it! An envelope, there on the table. I thought there was no need for farewells. It's been fun, hasn't it? You should call in one day … when we're settled. No need to see me off … my taxi will be waiting. The world is very small, don't you think? You understand, don't you?' And with that, Catherine departed for her train.

But Felicity follows to where she wasn't wanted, finds her friend in her compartment and waits on the platform for the train to leave.

As the train began its crawl, Catherine turns her suffering upon her friend … Felicity is shocked out of her sorrow. She smiles, tries to smile, smiles and reaches for the envelope with their money, smiles and waves, waves with a smile, waves goodbye.

In a great hubbub of metal and smoke the train disappeared into the night, leaving behind the farewellers who, even as the last carriage was cresting the end of the platform, were moving away into a new future … while Felicity sought out the comfort of a luggage trolley to sit, to think, to feel.

A voice was saying, 'What you got there, Missy?'

Felicity: 'It's only an envelope of money.'

'Oh Miss, you should'n play with that. You should put it somewhere safe. Now Miss, I needs ta'take this here trolley to where'its needed. So, if you'd mind putting yer feets up, and lean on the back like, I'll run you to the gate … like you was a Duchess, and off to the ball.' And as he pushed he sang, 'My father is king of the gypsies, it is true / My mother, she learned me some camping for to do / They put the pack all on my back, they did wish me well / So I set off to London town, some fortunes for to tell …'

Felicity arrives at the Manor Castlecrag to clean Lord Somersby's manor.

When his Lordship returns from his travels he finds a new roof on his manor, which was also in a fit and ready state … and less the cost of this resurrection from his bank account.

Chapter 12.
Pamela

For this final chapter I draw extensively from the last pages of Catherine's second journal and, where her text allows, I'll reproduce extended passages so you can hear one of our heroines in the first person.

These last entries were written in the 1960s, when Catherine was in her late seventies and living alone—her two children taken away by the second war and her husband by illness soon after war's end. Then aged and self-isolating, a dark fatalism attends her writing. Sleep was a parade of phantoms aboard a sinking ship, a black moon flickering invitingly amongst the ocean's slowly approaching cold and mysterious depths.

Catherine chanced upon a newspaper advertisement for the clearance of Castlecrag—the date, 'yet to be announced'. What motive sent her north I do not have to guess. She wanted to possess a painting of Felicity she knew hung in Castlecrag.

The house keeper takes a note to the master, explaining Catherine was a long-ago friend of the former Mistress, and would like to pay her respects and enquire of the clearance.

Ex-Lord Somersby, now George, comes to the vestibule to explain the clearance has been completed.

Catherine is taken aback, but says she was a friend of his mother, and knew his father; that she is interested in a painting, perhaps located in the library.

George Somersby's sunny disposition receives this as problematic.

'In the library,' admitting, 'there are paintings stored in the library. Just a collection of family portraits. Old boilers and sourpusses … a testimony to the family tradition of lives lived, not well.'

Catherine: 'I have visited here with your mother, in 1910, when she was a single girl. We came here determined to see the collection … in the library.'

'Let me introduce you to my sister, and the small party we are entertaining, then we will extricate ourselves for a chat. Perhaps you shouldn't mention the library or the painting, Mrs Broadhurst. It might unnecessarily distress my sister.'

The following is reproduced from the final pages of Catherine's second journal.

Mrs Verlaine Peabody-Somersby was a fair-haired grasshopper of a girl. Contentedly married, a delightful fortyish, fine-boned and flighty, completely unconscious of her sensuality. I wanted to tap her on the shoulder. The husband, a wealthy and happy American, was attentive and on point. After the pleasantries George and I withdrew to the library, chatting along the way. He has forsaken the title and was now George, joking George is not obsolete, and confided all had never been well between mother and daughter.

'I tried to understand it … she was father's girl. Doted on him. She cried like a baby at mother's funeral. It really knocked her about. There was nothing behind it, as far as I could tell. Mother was always trying. She resolved herself to trying. Mother wasn't … the most observant of social protocols. Now you know as much as I do.'

We found the library an empty shell. Still a beautiful aesthetic space, but now a graveyard of classical details, like a stage set without players, memories of memories of memories, and mine thrown in as if a ghost had walked onstage. Cabinets empty, the atlantes epic but lonely, and the light from the arched window streaming into nothing but the decorated bones of an empty room which use to be so interesting——that interest now winged its way to other heavens. Our adventure in Highgate came back to me like a wrecking ball. The George said 'Now, what were you looking for?' and I turned away to compose myself before admitting it was a painting of Felicity, apropos the collection.

My utterance stopped him so that he laughed. He descended several flights to my aged level, which was very polite, and said the collection had gone mostly as a job lot to a dealer in London—— quite lucrative, too——to be broken up and museumed. He looked at me sternly, but withdrew the examination as he handed me a catalogue of the collection, asked if I could spy the thing. I read as he talked——'I was fifteen when I first saw it. Father tried to explain it. At least I had a jump-start on my school chums'——but I couldn't find it. I said I knew it existed, while The George lounged on the windowsill as if he'd given up and was relieved at my failure.

I was at a loss … all I could think in this empty room was to visit the place where I knew it last to be, to touch the very place where I had been told the ridiculous work was hung, the walnut panels above the fire surround. By magic, with the slight pressure of my innocent hand, the panels sprang open, and there it was——a painting of the naked Felicity, as simpleton servant dusting a chandelier, the trick of a mirror revealing as much again, inviting the entire world to partake of her most raw possessions.

My host jumped to his feet, gasped, 'Oh Mother, really!' before bursting into laughter so intense he almost fell. He tried not to look at the image, but couldn't resist and collapsed again into laughter. Eventually saying, 'I dare not ask … but is this, the thing you are after?'

He then surrendered to a reverie, explaining how wonderful a mother she had been so that tears glazed his eyes as he spoke of her interest in her children and all that went on in their worlds. He said she always talked to them. 'Do you know, I have friends who have never had explained to them what selfishness is! They just do not know what it is, or what is loyalty or betrayal, or what is stealing, or even what it is to think. They know the words, but not the application. But mother always talked to us about such things.'

When his eulogy had burnt itself out I said it certainly was the thing I was after. He looked at me and I returned his gaze, hoping I didn't look like a defiant child. He said he'd fetch tea for us, and bring the things he would need to wrap my present.

I sat with my ghosts … and my next awareness was of an elderly woman materialising in the library's doorway. She looked cold and grey, as if a life of troubles had brought her to a state *of imminent collapse. She said something like, 'I knows you. You come with the Mistress, years ago. She told me … you married some fella … Mistress told me everything, she did. What you want here? What you after?'*

She was not as frightening as my dialogue might suggest. I mentioned the painting and for a moment her mind seemed to wander into utter sadness, but returned with, 'I don't know nothing 'bout no painting. But I knows things … I knows more than they knows. I knows what that town lady knows, see, but she don't know I knows.'

George arrived and shooed my visitor away, explaining every manor house has a Maud, and if they didn't they'd invent one. 'Maud came to the house as far back as I can remember. We used to call her Mad Maud, but mother put a stop to it. She can never finish a task, just wanders off and hides—behind furniture, in the garden, in cupboards. We had to lock the roof cavity … she was a foundling, spent her childhood in an orphanage.'

As he worked I tried to talk pleasantries while trying to make sense of a rising awareness, until he said jovially, 'Of course, Madame, there will be no charge for this.'

Then it came upon me, and it was my turn to feel the knife go deep into the heart, felt the heart beat against the cold blade. I couldn't speak for a time … I fear I must have looked a fright. He asked if I was all right. 'Yes,' I said, 'just something your mother said that has revisited me, from long ago.' But I was not all right … I was overcome with a terrible emptiness, as if I knew nothing about a past I had forsaken. I wanted to stay and I wanted to go. I said this had been a trial, 'seeing you and Verlaine. You must think I'm mad, the way I stare at you both. I just can't believe what I'm seeing.'

I corrected my presentation and regained some control, not wanting to drag him down with my pathos. He was off to New York and some kind of business when the property was sold, while his sister was returning to Texas. He said most passionately I should look him up if I was ever in New York, and made me solemnly promise.

I asked about his mother's life and he mentioned Pamela, a constant friend who lived in a bungalow on the edge of town not too far from there, and he gave directions that also passed Felicity's grave. While he would send the parcel to the station, I resolved to visit both on my progress back to the evening train.

~

Near the resting place of the Somersby's I saw Maud sitting on a rock, staring at the sky as if she were searching for a ship on that ocean's infinite and empty depths. My friend's grave lay behind an intricate iron fence, marked by a beautiful stone and scribed with fading gold lettering. Many years before, my friend protested the meaningless of such a place, yet I could not think she, who I loved and remembered so intimately, was now not so far away, stripped of warm flesh that was once something of passion and profound sentiment to me. I just could not make sense of my living memory reduced to grotesque and comic ruin.

My beautiful friend, who I would leave for the last time, leaving her to the bland sky and disinterested clouds, and the living affection from a confused mourner. The only touch of the living, a passing worm that bothered to pierce itself through my friend's dark earth.

I could not think this was the end of us while she still burned bright in my imagination. So I walked on, as the rain fell, as time walked with me, dissolving me as if it were acid.

I introduced myself as a friend of Felicity. Pamela's eyes seemed to vacate as another voice beyond asked who was there.

I entered into a bungalow of townie domesticity, a tight ship of order, of wide windows for the summer light and a comforting close ceiling to hold winter's fireplace warmth. The hostess betrayed herself with tight-wrung hands, while the host lounged in a chair, dressed to be staying in, and was of the kind who might know but *made it a business not to let on, a good mind irritatingly observant but gelded by an ease to be not anything.*

'Yes, Felicity spoke of you, the time she spent at The Grange. We often spoke, Felicity and I,' to which Gerald piped up, 'Inseparable, always conspiring, you and your Flick.'

'Hardly true, dear. I was never asked to the Manor's formal occasions, a blessing really, but it was her Arts Festival we planned, and sought to protect from the mayoral party. That brought us together. Not a success in the long run.'

Pamela wore the Contessa's bracelet on her wrist, wrapping her hand around it as if it was to be an object of contention. Our intercourse was wearing on Pamela—a late invitation to tea was the last thing she desired. Gerald started to fill a pipe and she bit at him, told him to go into the garden, which he did as unselfconsciously as a goat going to slaughter.

As I was making no sign of leaving, Pamela started talking about Felicity's Arts Festival, a subject she was comfortable with; gained confidence in her talk; said it was always a great success, they had traveller bands stay on the property ... 'Much criticism of that, but the people kept coming and the region's artists were over the moon with it all. Felicity was a wonder, how she encouraged, while knowing the terror of the truth. Much of it was painful. I remember a huge canvas, a landscape, set in the highlands. Must have taken years. You'd have to say the artist's ambitions overwhelmed his abilities. All the ingredients for disaster: scale, heroic clouds and distant snow-covered peaks … a muddy foreground with cattle. I think he dreamed it would hang in the Council Chambers.

'Felicity asked what I thought was the painting's subject.

'I said it was a painting of a bog. Felicity, pointing to a cow nearest the viewer, said it was about that cow's arse. We were rolling about the floor, just couldn't stop laughing.

'They formed a committee, to help. They thought they were so clever in taking away from her something she had brought to life, but they were nobodies, just opportunists, gossips, a group of panderers. Not a thought, not a right judgment amongst them. Just mean impulses, hanging together, concerned with getting whatever they thought they deserved! She just watched it towed away to the Town Hall to become a hulk. She amazed me … she just laughed, and then, nothing.

'You know, she didn't belong. I always hoped she'd ask me to go to Italy with her, but of course … it was just my daydream. She loved her children, was a great help to her husband. I was fortunate to know her. She deserved a quiet … easy passing.'

At this Pamela straightened, looked down at the hand covering the bracelet.

I watched as something horrible played about inside her.

I asked to be walked to the gate.

I offered my hand in farewell; she tentatively offered hers.

I held it, I did not let her go. Eventually panic overcame her, and a terror rose in her eyes, as if something awful was coming to the surface, as I refused to let go of her hand, the hand from which hung Felicity's bracelet.

Moments dragged like it must do at a hanging.

I saw her life draining away.

Eventually I released her. She gave a wounded cry, gasped for air and stumbled, fell backwards.

I turned to go through the gate and down the street to the station, and had a sense Pamela was stumbling away from me.

I don't know why I did it. I don't know what I felt.

The station was a half mile away. The day was overcast and drizzling, not a bird to give something living to the sky, a determined grumpy sullen misanthrope of a day. I thought of the worms underfoot—what a life!

The kind of noise that turns one's head had me staring at Pamela as she approached, walking at an odd angle, her head to one side, as if trying to understand. Eyes, staring and vacant, but the picture was of someone searching for an exit from a landscape of pain. She stopped before me in a most inhuman way ...

I find this too appalling. I have conveyed the substance of Pamela's testimony in my own voice, in the following.

Epilogue

I had all but delivered this novella when I was becalmed by a strange lethargy, as if a force was restraining me from sending my work hence.

Days passed as grim depression foiled any will to action.

Anyone who is weak enough to trifle with word-smithing has met the various crevasses that can open before one—writer's block is only the most named.

These interventions are assertive and mysterious, and I wonder if they are invited.

I assume these phenomena take a unique expression for each individual, but in your narrator's experience, finding a way forward has little to do with will or intellect. Apparently, I am allowed to cross over by a sign wholly unconnected to my own awareness. If one blunders on with brute force, waste and failure are the result, so one is liable to stop and wait for some … communication.

To venture an explication, are these Hamletesque delays caused by some intangible crisis of conscience, as if a ghostly concern stalks the dimly lit battlements of one's mind.

I have experienced other orders of writerly discontent. One lengthy example is paraded before the sensitive reader as my Apologia—a beast needing more than a year to hammer the argument into a form that describes its subject, and is, to my sensibility, only just adequate for my purposes, being still too indelicate and liable to stir up more damage to myself and the world than I wish.

Still musing about the vagaries of making text—cures seem to come providentially. I assume other writers have passages that are *not well*, textual *flats-spots* to my naming, places where I avert my eyes as if there lay a Medusa, hoping if I didn't acknowledge them, then who might?

One example of my literary cowardice was resolved in the following way—I dedicated a weekend to curing three lines of the flaws I had been denying for six months, but failing I resolved in Monday's dentist's chair to cut the blighters out. I returned to the work, and in thirty minutes had discovered a cure, and went on to apply the cure to a multitude of these *flat-spots*.

What caused this miracle?

The answer is, I just remembered what I had forgotten, that is all!

But then, what caused me to forget?

Please excuse my digression. Let me return to explaining how I overcame my *inertia* that restrained me from sending the story hence.

After many weeks of misery I realised my story was not finished. The revelation followed of something I had mentioned to you in passing, without seeing its potential. Can you guess what it might be?

It was the portrait the Contessa had arranged to be painted in Rome. Where was the painting now? If by a significant painter of the day it might be traceable. And would not its discovery be a poignant ending to my homage?

The Italian Consulate arranged for me to communicate with a fine arts librarian in Italy. I was offered just one possibility: an unnamed canvas known as *Le Ragazze Inglesi*, held in a gallery in northern Italy.

The excitement was taxing on my aging constitution— but how to get there, given my vow of poverty.

I'm afraid you, dear paragon of virtue, would, having learnt the addled facts, declared, 'Mountebank! I'll make sure you never again nun in this town!'

My straits compelled me to turn to a long ago ally, Sister Precious, who had been my guide during my novitiate. I knew she was ailing and might not recognise me, but I wished to see her for a last time—and if I had to beg, I knew Precious wouldn't make it humiliating, such was her nature.

Sister Bernadette, an abiding enemy from the Jurassic period, escorted me without chat to the hospice, and wanting our intercourse to be witnessed, I asked her to stay.

Sister Precious, my true friend, was tucked tight into her bed, a little dandelion gone to seed, with barely enough substance to resist the bed linen from releasing her piteous remains to the still air. Yet, the gentle irony that made me feel so valued and understood was strong and firm in her eyes—her eyes I remember as being polished orbs of obsidian, now turned a pearly grey

She seemed to recognise me, though I suspect her serenity might have smiled upon the dark lord if he happened by. I told her the story of Catherine and Felicity and, like a little miracle, she listened enraptured, as if this was the last adventure she would have in this world. I told her of my need … she thought … and like a benevolence watching over playing children, Sister Precious indicated a drawer and bade me take her gold cross.

I held it in my hands, then, 'It's not the one true cross …' and I knew Precious understood and was content.

Sister Bernadette and I knelt beside her bed and prayed for the soul of Sister Precious.

I knew we would not see each other again. I was escorted to the front gate, without chat, so I didn't bother either, being satisfied I had met my old friend and had received her bounty.

Arriving in late evening I found the hotel's barman to be a wealth of information about the Publico Galleria, which he described as an energetic cultural institution with a gang of ravens who hurry to the bedside of significant ailing citizens to remind them of the immortality they can achieve by a bequest to the Galleria. The Galleria, he said, is known for a significant collection of early-20th-century English works, and for an English language programme, including readings of Shakespeare.

When I heard this last, it did not resonate with me. He made an enigmatic statement I could only half-translate that was not at all *genial*, but before I could follow up he was called away, and that was that.

On a blustery winter's day I found the Galleria sitting big and a little inelegantly overlooking a little piazza.

The building was an 18th-century palazzo, a square box festooned with decorative elements and monumental columns thrown against its façade of three stories, with pleasingly ornate window surrounds streaming to left and right, and above, an attic story blocked out with square windows. A large Italian cornice crowns the roof line, casting a frown over the building. Austere iron gates and a little garden are both a serious and pleasant preparation to the Galleria and a reminder of its domestic antecedence, and something of a counterpoint to the piazza's businesses which seemed to offer laundry services and fortune telling. On entering, you find a light-filled salubrious space inhabited by a public library in one direction from the vestibule, and the Galleria in the other. A Café Pavilion is parked in the gardens behind, in a shady olive grove inhabited by marble satyrs.

But nothing in the world of dreams goes smoothly. Arriving I discovered the Galleria closed for renovation.

I sought the chief, with the humility of a nun who had been storing largesse under the veil, for the Parousia, but now was determined to spend this bounty in one gesture of secular vanity … only to be confronted by the chief, a young woman who was a duality of intelligence and youthful enthusiasm, and if I was to cast the Jesus story I would go no further than begging the image who stood before me to stand in for Mary Magdalene herself!

I stated my case urgently, highlighting the sensational and piquant aspects as if I was before the footlights.

Yes, they did have such a picture, a great favourite, a really fine portrait, and, she added, '*commovente*. I cannot explain. It came with little provenance but the wish it be on permanent display. If you don't mind walking through a building site …' I said it would be my pleasure, and had the oddest feeling I was being led by L'amministratrice to something more than a good painting, because she said to herself, and apropos whatever, '*Lo credo nei miracoli.*'

Thinking now I'd better keep an eye on her I ventured, 'And do you remember the donor's name?'

'*Sì.*'

Her diffidence annoyed me. She knew very well my interest.

'Was it Vasari? Perhaps Contessa Polissema de Vasari?'

'*Vicino*. Contessa Polissema Jacobs. She married briefly British ambassador, in Roma. She was too much fun. I hope you can offer interesting background to this work, if it is what you seek. Perhaps we can both gain something … if you are brave, Sister … to take a bit of local … ah, *politica*.'

We stood looking up at the most wonderful painting. A picture, not grand in scale, but large enough to be a careful examination of two girls on a sofa, their backs to a large window, the brown-haired girl reading a book, while the fair other rests against her with her arm linked through the reader's while examining the bracelet on her wrist. The composition so simple, and yet the execution was exceptional and invited examination.

I couldn't help myself exclaiming, 'The bracelet that the Contessa gave Felicity! It's described in Catherine's journal!' and tears began to fill my eyes, seeing their life, seeing their friendship, this memento of a friendship that lasted until their end.

My host commented she had often tried to decipher the book's title. I said a note in Catherine's journal identifies it as Ovid's *Amores*.'

My host gasped, and said that is very amusing.

I couldn't take my eyes off the fineness of the work— the distance through the window was exquisite, so finely done it seemed to reverberate back to the principals. In fact, the window's distant view had a slightly more serious tone that caused a subtle disjuncture from the girls, as if, perhaps, the artist had fated them to the transcendent distance and what was to be.

'And what are their names? We don't have information about this picture. It was … the painter was a prodigy who had fallen out of favour.'

I noted my guide's difficulties in composing this utterance and it occurred to me whatever was being obscured might manifest later. I replied, 'The reader is Catherine Dewhirst. Her friend is Miss Felicity, she had no family name, she was a natural child. They came to Italy as romantic adventurers.'

'And what happened to them, Sister?'

It was time for placing all on the table. Some of the following will be new to a reader, and is produced here from the last scene with Pamela.

'Catherine wrote suffragette tracts for a English newspaper, in 1910, about the experience of Continental women. The Contessa Vasari befriended the girls in Florence, and in Rome she had them sit for this portrait. They were deported from Italy as revolutionaries, or anarchists. Of course, they were nothing of the sort. Just girls who accidently worked the system and were caught out by the authorities. They were returned to England at the end of the year, parted … They never met again. You could say Catherine ran out on her friend, but that's how some things end.

'Felicity, the girl examining her bracelet, went north, to clean an aristocrat's house. By the time he came back from travel his house was in order, with a new roof, and he was a good deal poorer. He became enamoured of her. There were two children. Later she fell so ill her jewellery bruised her skin by their gentle weight. Her life was ended by a friend who couldn't stand her suffering. The housekeeper retrieved her jewellery and the bracelet was given to her friend. She wore it.'

I heard my guide gasp. I told the rest of what Pamela had told Catherine during that dreadful encounter, about Algy and Felicity, about the children being theirs. That Algy lost his life as a medic in 1918.

Catherine's husband had given up his political career to marry her, both their children lost in the second war, and Catherine's husband soon after. I told of Catherine's journey to Felicity's house to retrieve the painting … how she saw the bracelet featured in the painting, on Pamela's wrist.

'Soon after, she hung herself … whether it was the bracelet, the painting, or just circumstances that sent her over, I cannot tell.'

'Oh, Sister. What a tragedy!'

We looked at the picture for some time and agreed it made us happy to know it was appreciated by the public.

L'amministratrice invited me to lunch, said she'd like to get the details of my story. And so we walked about town, found a deserted café and sat in a warm corner sizing each other up. She asked about my life and I told her some of the things I've told you, mainly those things stated in my Apologia … which I am sure you read without warmth.

She was a very glamorous girl with an air of restraint that spoke to me of discipline, thoughtfulness, and interest in the world she moved through. I didn't envy the long road that lay before her.

She was starting on a career of libraries and galleries, and seemed to grow younger the more we talked. Then L'amministratrice confessed to a subterfuge, one which I have noted above I suspected.

She had not spoken all that was true and relevant— the palazzo was the Contessa's last home; she had donated the building to house the Galleria and library, and was responsible for building the English collection and the English language programme. The Contessa's bequest had been left to an administrator to fulfil in the 1960s—a White Russian émigré, Miss Nadenka Stern, who was feared and hated, and was thought to be insane. It seems Stern's administration embraced the popular culture of the sixties, fulsomely.

I must know, L'amministratrice said, the eternal attraction of exercising power ... that forces were massing against the Galleria that had already overpowered the frailties of the library. The new manager had dismissed key roles, reduced the authority of those below the manager, and the newly hired were beholden. They were attempting to 'rationalise' the whole palazzo, she said.

'It will be no surprise to you, Sister, to know the beneficiary of the new order will be the sponsors of it. I was hired because they thought I could be handled … There is no stopping the tide, but I think the Galleria has enough for one last blast of fun … and who knows, perhaps that will be enough to get past this latest enthusiasm.'

L'amministratrice spoke carefully, as one stepping on stones to cross a stream, 'They want the Galleria … but they don't want the Contessa. They don't like her politics, her lifestyle … and they don't like her Shakespeare. She was arrested in the '30s and imprisoned for a time, but the clergy rescued her. The family paid her off with the palazzo and some money. They wanted to ride the black wave … and disappeared when the tide went out. She is buried not far from here. Perhaps we can visit after our coffee?'

I said I'd like that very much.

Then L'amministratrice sprang her little trap. 'I have her papers. Part of my custodial duties. They are safe in bank vault. What a story! And the goings-on in the '60s … Stern was responsible for that. I can tell you, Sister, the Galleria rocked a few ancient ruins! Once, the local left and right each made a plan to burn down the palazzo, but they discovered the other's plan and each reported it to the police. Hilarious! Like that American comedy team, you know … with the confused immigrant and the cynical bourgeois … but not the empyreal one … Oh yes … there are letters from an English Catherine.'

The shock went right through me. I must have looked very stupid before I managed, 'Any letters are outside my interest, regarding my novella. I certainly don't want to be a voyeur, or a busybody.'

'Sister … you wouldn't be a voyeur if you were biographer. Would you?'

I could not reply as temptation wrestled with nothing. She continued, referring to my teaching years; said she was seeking an educator, fluent in English, part of the schools program, and based on the collection, but also some out-of-school hours, speaking and writing. Not too lucrative, but adequate, she thought. 'I wonder, Sister, if you would be interested in such a position?

'You would see a lot of me. I'm in need of an ally. I have a publisher who is impatient for a start. Biography would put the Contessa centre stage, a foil to the ambition of the managers. They have made efforts to control the papers … I can only promise two more years before I move. I cannot afford to make enemies of them. If we get the Contessa on her pedestal, I think her influence will be assured. We have citizens committee. They are sleepy, but would wake with violence if they thought a local girl was being mistreated. And if things go to our plan … how about a bronze of our girl … a welcoming Contessa at our garden gate?'

There was a lot to think about as we walked in silence along narrow time-worn streets to the cemetery. I did not ask my L'amministratrice what she was thinking, but I was thinking of Rick Blaine's *hill of beans.* Soon we arrived at the tiny plot hosting the remains of the Contessa Polissema de Vasari.

It would not be difficult to correctly guess the sentiment in English written on her headstone.

We passed the time in silence, I, for my part, surrendering to the cold sunshine and birdsong and to whatever was inhabiting my companion, and soon it came, a subtle unwinding of tension I dared not turn my head to witness, as she said, 'I wonder, Sister. Did she like both girls, equally?'

Although I could have done with a laugh, I restrained myself, and mustered a mature tone for my reply.

'She only had eyes for Catherine,' and I felt my Mary Magdalene blush.